38 Shirts

A new collection of distinctive s

Contents -

1. 38 Shirts
2. The Puppet that Pulled Back
3. Martin's New Year
4. Life at the top
5. Human Obsolescence

6. Job Description for a Human Being
7. X1Vth Annual International Security Conference
8. By The Christmas Tree
9. Welcome to the Ministry of Defence
10. You Lucky Boy!

11. Spiritual Roadside Assistance
12. Jack and Me (his Dad)
13. Landing on The White House Lawn
14. What role a Man?
15. A Very Personal Lockdown

1. 38 Shirts

He'd had a rather pleasant day, as it had turned out. His official and very proper office calendar had said that he would be "Working from Home" and he had indeed done some good work from home, quite a lot in fact. He had been a very productive boy all that morning, starting real and proper work at 7.05 am according to the clock on his ageing Blackberry, and steadily working through all of the new incoming e-mails that had come through into his mailbox overnight by just after 7.35 that morning.

He went downstairs to make a fresh cup of tea, always regular breakfast tea and never Earl Grey tea for him, patting his loyal chocolate Labrador Sienna on the head on his way through to the kitchen. She was let out into the garden for a morning wee. Meanwhile he made his first pot of tea of the day, let the dog back into the family room shortly afterwards, and took his mug of hot tea back upstairs to his familiar office. He felt rather smug that he had been dedicated enough to his job to have read through his e-mails already, even before pouring another cup of tea - probably before anyone else in the firm had even taken a look at their e-mail. He felt good about that and he winked at himself in the mirror high up on the wall, by way of a little self-praise and encouragement.

He didn't remember the last time that he had done that, not the winking thing in the mirror high up on the wall but the self-praise thing.

The rest of the family were just stirring in their various bedrooms, and he just got on with sending a few more emails and making some quick notes online on the company's CRM system, just as long as he had that little bit of personal quiet time left to him. The internet connection seemed very good today, and he had made some further good progress by eight am. His tea tasted good, a little strong perhaps, but the day was definitely getting off to a good start. That was always a nice feeling on any day, but it felt particularly reassuring on a Friday.

His very lovely wife Hermione was soon up as well, showered and drying her short blonde hair to go off to her place of work. She worked for a major American consulting firm, as she liked to tell anyone who would listen to her, and the business of getting ready in the morning to "look the part" was not an inconsiderable one, as the whole family had grown to learn. He went back downstairs to make her a cup of her preferred Earl Grey tea. Generally, it was advisable that she was not to be more than very lightly interrupted from her important pre-office preparations. A cup of her favourite tea was acceptable to her, but it was not always drunk completely he had noticed, unlike at the weekends.

Three envelopes were posted through the door by their friendly postie Dennis.

By eight fifteen, their three children had also been up and about, all of them had got dressed and had set off to their various schools. They would all be back home safely by about five pm that evening, one of them by car and two on foot. The assertive, overpowering and well-dressed Hermione had also left by now, leaving through the front door already doing business on her phone of course, probably closing some kind of high-level deal with an impressive financial Client somewhere in a superficial, glitzy city, somewhere. Her expensive eyebrows did the job of connecting visually, only momentarily mind you, with her husband of some twenty years now, and somehow saying "Goodbye, see you later, have a nice day, don't forget to pick up my dry cleaning for the party tonight, and I absolutely promise to be back home in time to change for the party and to get there by eight pm", all in just a single raise of one mascara-decked eyebrow. Quite a powerful thing that, to be able to do all of that in so short a period of time, don't you think? It was rather clever too on his part he often thought to take such a lot of meaning from so simple and hard a gesture first thing in the day.

But he was well used to it by now, very much used to it all.

He had already shaved and showered very early by now, and changed into his "WFH" clothes, which were really nothing more than a very loose pair of track suit trousers that he wore to go running in the winter on only the very coldest of nights, together with a navy blue Ralph Lauren polo shirt. This was originally one size too large for him when first bought for him by the overbearing Hermione, but which now fitted him very well. So much for the high quality Ralph Lauren label saying that this garment would most definitely not shrink in the wash! It had but in this case for the better. Not an entirely stylish outfit but genuinely really comfortable for working from his light and airy home office.

A pair of light great and very inexpensive Donnay running socks would complete his "WFH" look that day, and he felt really very comfortable in it all. No prizes for sartorial style of course but there again that did not matter to him when working alone at home. A light breakfast of a banana, a vanilla flavoured yoghurt and single piece of wholemeal toast, with three fruits marmalade, set him up nicely for the day and he worked through some more emails and a couple of slightly tedious conference calls throughout the morning. His progress had been good to start with, very good, but Robert knew from previous experience that his work rate was extremely high for the first few hours of the day, and that it then started to decline pretty steadily up until around that time of day that we often call "lunchtime".

He therefore needed to really crack through the important stuff as early on as possible. Prioritisation and all that, as he had learned so many years ago on his first time management workshop from the famous Filofax organisation, was simply critical if things were going to get done.

By midday, his work rate was really very poor. He was starting to slow down by then. If he had been in the company office working at that rate, his boss would most likely have come over and asked what the hell he was playing at. More tea was made, some bland post in official looking envelopes was opened, a couple of incoming sales calls were taken on his home office line, that's if pre-recorded robotic phone calls can ever be described as true sales calls. They certainly weren't that in Robert's book, and as soon as he heard that tell-tale pause on the line he knew that it was Mr or Mrs Robot, again! The receiver would go down on the caller almost immediately but it frustrated him because it broke his concentration and that was not fair. Not fair on him. You see, fairness was an important concept for him, always had been. That and trust.

A little after one pm, when making yet another cup of tea in the kitchen area, his eyes had connected with those of Sienna, the family's chocolate Labrador. Gorgeous dog, Like it had happened earlier with his wife's seriously professional eyes, so many significant things were to be communicated in so short a space of time between the two of them that it was hard to believe. Things for example like...

"I know that you are a very busy human, and that you need to earn something you call money to pay for the lovely house that we all live in, but might you possibly be able to find some of that thing that you people call "Time" and take me for a little walk? Please.

Any time today would be good, really, but since we are talking about the topic right now, just the two of us here, and that since you are not actually working and appear to be on some kind of official break, would sometime soon be possible, before you go back upstairs? Like now? Please. Really? Oh good, I'll put that cute puppy look on my face that you like so much with my soft furry ears pushed forward and go and stand by the front door, in great expectation. I will wag my tail enthusiastically too. Like I did yesterday, and that day before that. And the day before that too".

Quite a powerful thing that to be able to do that in so short a period of time don't you think? It was rather clever too on his part he often thought to take such a lot of meaning from so simple a gesture first thing in the day. But then this man had both a sharp mind and an imagination, quite a rare combination in the male of the species.

And so yet another dog walk was had. It wasn't a long one but Sienna had got a good forty minutes of running around and chasing the ball. He had one of those big red plastic ball throwers that helps you to throw the ball a very long way by giving you the thrilling opportunity to throw your dog's ball in a much wider arc than you can by throwing it just by hand. Robert once wondered if it worked with assertive wives too. Definitely worth a try though one day.

And it certainly worked very well, for Sienna must have been sent off on at least thirty separate missions to get the ball, thus increasing significantly the distance that she actually covered in their forty minutes together. He, the man, had a good lunchtime walk too of course, but the dog had travelled way further, and that was all that mattered, that and taking his iPhone with him to "stay in touch" with the working world. But no-one had called or sent him any mails that lunchtime, probably because it was a Friday and many people were out at the pub or somewhere similar having lunch together. He was a little disappointed if the truth be known at how quiet it was in that particular department.

Back home, the Labrador was given some fresh water and a few little dog biscuits by way of a treat. Part of the deal here between man and dog was that she would have to sit down on her big brown dog bed to dry off and stay sat there for quite some time, in order to get the biscuits from him. She was wet from somehow always finding some water along the way to play around in. They had a system between them you see, and they both knew how it worked by now. She was fine with her part of their human-canine deal, and he felt a little virtuous too afterwards. Good little system. He scratched her back and she his.

Instead, of going back to his office, he took a cup of tea upstairs and unusually walked straight past the office and into their bedroom. Placing the mug on his tall bedside chest of drawers, he went over to his wardrobe just to get his clothes out for the party later that evening, and to do nothing more. As is so often the case, he had not even seen his dinner jacket in twelve months, not since the last black tie party that they had been invited to this time last year, and he hoped that it was still good enough to wear.

You see, men's dinner jackets are famous for mysteriously shrinking in size over the year since their last annual outing.

No-one really knows how it happens, not truly, or why, but every twelve months middle-aged men all up and down the country are in no doubt whatsoever that this is a very real and a very strange phenomenon. It just happens for some reason annually. You'd think that the clothing stores would launch a big public investigation into the issue, particularly Marks and Spencer, but they never actually had and their only response seemed to be to make lots of new dinner jackets in all kinds of sizes, year after year, and generally in black. Somewhere in there, hanging deep within that long wardrobe too was his smart dress shirt. Now that really did have to be completely clean for tonight he thought. A black dinner jacket can pass okay with a small wine stain from last year somewhere on the material if you sit strategically enough, but a good white dress shirt needs to be one colour and one colour only. White is white after all, and nothing else would do.

In searching for this formal garment, he felt a strange sensation come over him very suddenly, but really odd, like he had never experienced before. It was sufficiently strong to stop him from looking any further for his dress shirt for quite some time. He simply stopped looking for anything or even doing anything, and he stood utterly still.

He was without any movement. A motionless man.

His body didn't even sway, not in the slightest. It was like his feet were bolted to the floor, and forever. Only his eyes could move, and his head stayed in the same position, as he just looked ahead deep into his long, white wardrobe.

There was a reason for this behaviour you see. He just couldn't believe how many shirts he had. That was what was making him freeze. Just that realisation on its own, nothing else. And it didn't feel good.

He was experiencing guilt. And he thought that he could also sense a little dizziness.

Just how many shirts did he have these days? He had to count them, he couldn't not, and so he would.

Shirt number one was at the far end to his left and he started counting from there, back down the line in his direction towards where he was standing. One, two, three, four, five, six, seven, eight, nine, ten, eleven, ...eighteen, nineteen, twenty, twenty one, twenty two..... twenty nine, thirty..... he was down onto the lower level now, thirty one, thirty two, thirty three, thirty four, thirty five, thirty six, thirty seven, thirty eight.

Shit!

He had thirty eight shirts, and they were all just for this one man. Not thirty eight shirts you understand for the entire road that he lived in, or for all of the men in the whole village, or to be shared amongst the male population of the county, but just for him. For Robert. Thirty eight bloody shirts. Just for him. For one man only. Him. All in his size. Thirty eight. He had thirty eight shirts, just for him. Thirty eight shirts for just one man.

How many shirts does a man need? Not this number for sure he thought, and still the metal bolts through his feet were keeping him fully in place, unable to move though the shock of it all.

He had a total of thirty eight shirts. Thirty eight, and he had just counted them all.

By now the original task of looking for one specific and hopefully very white dress shirt had now vanished from his head totally. Instead all that was there was a whole heap of ugly guilt. He felt a feeling that he could not ever remember having experienced before. A moral sickness. That stemmed from him having two less than forty shirts. He had become a man who owned thirty eight shirts.

Images of an African village with some poorly dressed people, wandering around in the heat of the day came into his mind. These were mental images of a faraway people who did not even have one good shirt to wear on their young backs, not one each. Let alone two or three, let alone again the guilty figure of thirty eight. Thirty eight bloody shirts. The vast continent of Africa had suddenly made an appearance into his Berkshire home, and the wardrobe was his window into a very different world. A world that he felt he should at least care about, not that everyone in Berkshire did of course. But he knew that he definitely should.

"How could this dreadful thing have happened?"

he asked in a whispered voice, but literally saying out loud, loud enough for all thirty eight to have heard what he had just said.

How could he have allowed the just absurd number of thirty eight shirts to build up in his one wardrobe? Thirty eight bloody shirts. We have only one back to wear our shirt on he thought, but somehow he had amassed the ludicrous figure of thirty eight shirts to cover it. That was a ratio of thirty eight shirts to one back. Thirty eight bloody shirts. He wondered what the more common shirt to back ratio was amongst other middle-aged males. Thirty eight separate pieces of Egyptian cotton cloth, all with bright, shiny buttons on them. That was enough to last him nearly eight weeks at work without having to wash or iron a shirt! Thirty eight bloody shirts. Enough for nearly two months. He had become the man who had thirty eight shirts.

This was not good.

In fact is was nothing less than absurd.

The steel bolts through his feet had started to loosen very slightly now and they allowed him to step back just a little from this very serious situation and to start to take it in more fully. He shook his head, literally in disbelief at what he had just found in his own house, in his own home, and in his own wardrobe. Thirty eight bloody shirts. He thought that maybe he should draw a thick white chalk line round his bedroom wardrobe, after all that was what they did in a crime scene wasn't it? For this definitely felt like a crime to him, and he Robert was right in the middle of it. Yes, he felt like a dirty criminal, that was exactly it. Not because he had stolen the shirts from a department store or anything like that, but for an entirely different reason, because no man needs thirty eight shirts! Does he? Not thirty eight bloody shirts, surely? Even his hero the wonderful Barack Obama surely never had that number in his wardrobe, even as The President? Eight maybe, ten perhaps, possibly a dozen, conceivably fourteen, just possibly up to twenty for all of those days of public announcements and interviews and foreign territory visits, but never as many as Robert had, surely? No, not thirty eight, he was certain of that.

Robert the modern and well-dressed criminal … As a kid he was always fascinated by the fact that his name had the word "robber" within it, albeit slightly misspelt. Perhaps it was all turning out to be true now after all of those years, for he felt certain now that he was taking shirts off the backs of people whose need was patently greater than his.

Hmm, this was now a significant problem in his life. His whole day was now affected by this sad discovery. This was not something that he could just forget, for every time that he opened his wardrobe doors the evidence of fine Egyptian cotton would be only too plain to see. Every time that he put a shirt onto his middle-class, middle-aged British back so he would feel the associated guilt. He imagined a large black number that would appear on the bedroom wall to confirm exactly what number shirt he was wearing that day, a bit like a huge counter on the wall confirming that "Yes, today's shirt was number 17 of 38 Robert, and you still have a further 21 shirts available to you and your middle-class back".

That's okay he thought, as he sought to justify it all, it's okay to know your number if you play in a football team but not if these are just ordinary, everyday shirts that you are taking out of a wardrobe.

Thirty eight bloody shirts. This had become mad to somehow have amassed so many.

Hmm, he even thought about packing say half of them up and putting them into a white plastic charity clothes bag to drop off at the clothes bank later that evening. That would lessen the guilt a little, probably, and if anyone was to come round and march him up to his wardrobe and throw the doors open, at least a lesser total of nineteen shirts would be easier to own up to than thirty eight! Surely the moral police would be okay with that? After all, nineteen is less than twenty and it's not quite enough for one full and busy month of shirt wearing anyway, assuming that you wear a nice clean one each and every day. Which he did.

Brainwave time! A moment of inspiration, how clever! He tried compressing them so that they took up only half of the space in the wardrobe, but still that number of 38 loomed down on him from the bedroom wall shirt counter, and in deep, darkest black ink too.

And so he moved them back to where they were, so as not to leave them all creased. There now really looked to be no escaping the fact that he was the guilty owner of thirty eight shirts, it was plain and simple. Mind, not all the shirts were plain, some were checked or striped, but his crime was plain and simple. He recognised that.

Another thought rushed into his head. For his mind had moved from shirts to ties, and from ties onto belts and trousers and then onto shoes next. Cufflinks too, and then there were all of his socks, and his boots, not to mention all of his jackets and autumn fleeces and several coats downstairs too. He owned three raincoats as well. Three! For just one man. At least four pairs of gloves too! Yet, he only had two hands like most other people did. He knew that he had a collection of ties that was pretty well-known back in the office, and that he had a reputation amongst his colleagues and customers too, for always wearing very high quality silk ties, always bought from the very best gentlemen's shops in Jermyn Street. And then there were the jeans, he had at least ten, maybe a dozen pairs of them, easily, and they were not cheap jeans either. "Kosher" they were. Some in black, but mostly in blue.

Then there were Chinos too, he always bought at least two or three pairs when he was over in the US on business, and they were neatly folded away in another completely separate cupboard in their spare bedroom! Worse than that was that they were stacked according to their shade of beige, from light to medium to dark, now that was truly sick! Some he had never worn, not even once – gulp! How bad was that? What the hell was he doing buying more chinos just because they cost less in the US than they did in Europe, but when he didn't ever wear chinos?! Pratt. He had got to a point in his life then when he was spending good money on things that he would never wear and which he absolutely did not need. The moral police would surely take a strong interest in his impressive and unused collection of chinos, little leniency would be shown there he thought. He could see the newspaper headlines already.

Moments of comparison with Hermione's clothes collection skipped through his mind. Her shoes and business suits were legends in their own lunchtime, numerous silk scarves too, as well as handbags, but they didn't stay long in his mind because he couldn't shake off his own "big issue" that needed addressing immediately. He had amassed thirty eight shirts, and like his chinos, some of those had never been worn. And he knew exactly which ones too. It was almost as though they were bought purely to be shown off to deeply shallow people passing by his wardrobe, rather than to be actually worn. "Drive-by shirt admirers", he thought, now what a sad idea that was! Which was sadder though, other people seeing his shirt collection or him having the thirty eight shirts in the first place? Probably the latter he concluded.

What did a man's selection of shirts actually say about the man behind them anyway, he considered. What knowledge of a man could be gleaned from a quick glance through his bedroom wardrobe? More importantly, what did his own shirts say about him? All thirty eight of them that was. Still, he was unable to process that number in his mind. He was sure that he couldn't have gone out and bought them all, surely not? Not a many as thirty eight.

You could say that he had all manner of styles and patterns in his collection, and that was certainly how it looked at first glance. But a more careful look showed something slightly different going on there. There were three main styles to Robert's shirts you see – strong plain colours for work, fine striped ones again for work, and then numerous checked ones that were for casual wear only, and sometimes for dress-down days at his place of work.

What did this selection say about him he pondered, what conclusions would be reached about Robert through others studying his collection of shirts...? Well, probably that he appeared to be a very conservative man first of all, and that he wanted the present world order to stay just how it was. His shirts suggested that he was against any change or revolution, that he supported the Pope in his heavenly white gowns, and the whole Christian religion Belief thing that he headed up. The blues and the striped shirts also seemed to imply that he supported all of the wars in Iraq just on principle alone, and that he considered civilians who got in the way as "legitimate collateral damage", and that he enjoyed the company of US neo-conservatives across the dinner table, that he drank fine red wine and ate red meat at least five times a week, sometimes every day. These were surely the shirts of a man that drove the very latest German cars only, and a man too that had his pension already sorted out by the time he was thirty nine, (one number greater than his thirty eight shirts), and that he was a full and unashamed monarchist, who probably disapproved of people who were gay, and that he thought that abortion was tidy and for the best, and too that a woman who was raped had been asking for it, and that no Muslim could ever be trusted, ever, anywhere, under any circumstance, and that you really were either for the government or against them when it came to terrorism, and that 9/11 was exactly how the media had chosen to position it, like one hundred per cent, nothing different, and that there were no other species of intelligent life anywhere in the universe, none at all, and that people who said there were should be quickly locked up and the key thrown away, forever, and that the entire universe had been created by a tall, slim white middle-class God educated at Cambridge University called Jeremy, and that everyone should be privately educated, (weren't most anyway), and that the world was here for us to use up and enjoy, sod the next generation, (or generations plural), and that it was entirely acceptable and even logical for us all to base our lives on the "carpe diem" principle only, and to just "go for it", and that there was nothing more to human existence than the optimization of your pleasure, that financial hedonism was entirely justified in all situations, that every man owned a Rolex wristwatch by the time that they were thirty five, and that by mid-forties he had this thing called "Life" nearly sussed. Oh, and yes, one other little point, the NHS idea was probably quite a good thing, originally as a nice idea, but don't we all actually both think and know that it can also be a "bottomless pit" into which money could be poured, our hard-earned money too that is, so let's just rein it back in as much as we can. You good with that? After all, Private Hospitals are so much nicer inside, actually very pleasant places, don't you think, with nice fresh flowers and the staff are so pleasant to you too? They're trained professionally in that way, you see. Good coffee machines too, even Nespresso ones, like George Clooney drinks.

Thirty eight bloody shirts, all his after all hanging up for all to see, and that is almost certainly what they said about him to anyone passing by his collection. What they said about the man behind these thirty eight shirts. Thirty eight, how was this possible, how had it happened, and to him?

Oh My God.

But you see, and do please understand this, that wasn't how Robert was. No, not at all. He was very different to this, really very different indeed. And he knew this "deep down", so that made him feel just a little better. A little less evil perhaps. Robert, evil wasn't ever his thing, no not Robert.

Actually, he was of course a Socialist first of all. The Principles of Socialism sat well with him, and really well. They had done ever since he had worked in a large NHS hospital in South East London when he was in his early twenties and as far as he knew, he had not met any neo-Conservatives either. And he was proud that it was his Labour party that came up with the NHS under their Health Minister Aneurin Bevan in the first place. He considered it a truly great achievement in fact, not just "a nice idea" like the other man behind his shirts might have. So, there you go, that was how Robert thought about good things like that.

Did he want Revolution? Well, do you know, that was an interesting question now. Yes and then again No. He didn't want an "On the Street kind of Revolution" no, not a socially dangerous or restless ongoing kind of revolution. Not one that endangered Human Life, but he did want many things to change in general, and so in a general sense he wanted another kind of revolution. He wanted us to wake up to the Climate Emergency.

And for the record, he thought that Greta Thunberg was a pretty remarkable young woman who had nothing other than the very best of motives. She should be praised and supported, and above all she should be listened to. After all, that teeny weeny word "Emergency" was a bit of a clue, don't you think? We were now living at what could literally be a Tipping Point for the Human Species, and sadly for so many others on this planet too. He also rejected the notion that this was "Our Planet", preferring instead the recognition that we were fortunate enough to have been given Life on it, and that came in the form of a temporary Access Pass only. Temporary, yes? Our ignorance with regard to our impact on the Climate and the environment in general was little less than breath taking, and we needed a full-on revolution in that area for one, yes. Greta for President then! And the sooner the better….

When it came to Religion, he wasn't the best man to engage with, not if you wanted a lengthy and informed debate. For his knowledge of the World that is manmade Religion was comparable to his knowledge of the World of Wine. He knew that there is White Wine and there is Red Wine. Oh, and yes there is a rather nice one called Rose wine too, and they all come from grapes, somehow. So, there is Islam, and there is Christianity and there are some others too, but there's also a box that you can tick which says "None of the Above". That would be the one that he would tick. He had no problem with people choosing which Team they followed, the white guy or the brown guy's religion, either could be their choice. He just didn't go with either option, and that was because his Mind didn't seem to go down that kind of Path, well not naturally anyway. He was much more open-minded in that regard. What did get his goat, even thought he was a committed Pescatarian, was the idea of one team ramming their Game Strategy down the throats of anyone else. No, that was just not acceptable to him, and that was not good in so many ways, and on so many levels. We're all here for a possible reason, and the rules that he preferred to play by were those of Respect, Tolerance and a healthy dose of Understanding. He thought it pretty unlikely that one team actually understood what that reason might be better than the other guys, and so what mattered was T for Tolerance. Have your viewpoint, yes, and if you come from a gang that shares that viewpoint then fine, but let's not take the Higher Ground based on what is essentially nothing more than a guess. F for Faith is fine, but not F for FuckUp. Not for him the white and apparently superior whiteness of The Vatican, thankyou very much. And whatever secrets they had been hiding in there for hundreds of years.

And talking of Wars … nor did he subscribe to the view that Mankind was essentially a warmongering species naturally. Yes, there was a level of fight and aggression in us naturally, and probably a fair dose of what might be called Tribal Aggression too, but that could operate on a very low level really, if only we could see that. Competition is okay, but not Dominance or Dictatorship. What we also had the opportunity to do was to rise to a higher level of Consciousness and be a better species, which he believed absolutely we could do. If we could just stop the primitive thugs of this world running the show quite so often using things like violence, arms, money, secrecy and false arguments, then we could go onto bigger, and brighter and better things. On a higher level, and he really did believe that it was up there. We just had to find it.

And here was the interesting thing… that just might include all of us. Even the thugs, they had a part to play in the Higher Game. Clearly, clearly, there had been no Weapons of Mass Destruction. What a surprise! Hans Blick from The United Nations knew that, you knew that and the bloke in the pub knew that. If it was true, the war was long-planned in advance and Bush and his poodle Blair were going to go in, come who or what may. And this was one of the things in Life that saddened him most. For Robert could almost not countenance the suggestion that Wars were planned years in advance. What kind of Human Being would even take part in that as an activity?! Think of the hospitals that you could build. And the schools too. Or the vaccines to Pandemics, current and potential, that could be found. Think of the litter that could be swept up from the World's great Oceans, and the improvements in the quality of the air that we breathe that could be prioritised over …. Going into a War.

The outgoing President Harry S. Truman was completely right when he warned the US public in 1953 to beware the increasing influence of the "Military Industrial Complex". He was right, and tragically in his mind, the rest was history. Imagine having just ten per cent of the funds that had been spent in War over the past one hundred years, he sometimes thought, and what Good might be done with it. How inspiring would that be? Very, he concluded.

So, no, not Mainstream Religion for him, and certainly not going into War, let alone planning them in advance. How could any of those Monsters even sleep knowing the extent of innocent Civilian casualties in the Gulf Wars that they had fucking planned? And then there was Monarchy, and you really didn't want to get him going on that one! Where in God's name had that one come from? Not from God that was for sure, even though they invoked the hilarious notion of a "Divine Right!" You see for him that was simply wrong on both counts. And the notion that some people were superior in some way to others just plain offended him. He actually thought further that it was an affront to the intelligence of the ordinary man, you know, the ones that the Controlling Team were happy to send to their deaths in senseless wars. The ones that came under the collective title of "Cannon Fodder". What a nightmare for good and healthy Young Men, millions of them, like his own son. He was a healthy heterosexual man but give him a Queen any day to HM The Queen. People should surely be allowed to be themselves, regardless of their sexuality, their age, their religious views, their preferred style of relationship, their profession, their ethnicity, their gender preference, and so on…. See what he meant about finding that Higher Level?

It was up there all right, they just had to find it.

From his reading on the subject nor had 9/11 been what Bush and Cheney wanted the World to think it was. Sadly, the Ordinary Man and Woman had a remarkable ability to behave like sheep so often and here was an example. An utterly prime example too. When searching for The Truth he had found that you have to make a decision to be uncomfortable for some time in that search. Even if it was a lengthy one. Most people sadly went for The Comfy Option, which of course the Thugs knew they would. They were right about that, they had done their prep, they knew how the group thinking would go, and the masses just relinquished their ability to think independently, when being part of the herd was just so much easier.

The Truth was that there was so many things that he wanted to understand better. For this man, this man of thirty eight shirts, was curious and hungry. A simple man but very curious for explanations about many things. And the notion that his fellow man could be so deceitful and dishonest disappointed him greatly, when just a slight movement of the points on the train track could have sent them all down a path of Honesty and Transparency. You understand don't you, on a path towards the Higher Level Stuff that he simply craved.

He left both of the white wardrobe doors open, both completely wide open in fact and as far as their brass hinges would allow, with the thirty eight pieces of clear evidence on full view, and went downstairs briskly to find the free white plastic bags that the charity organisations put through your letter box from time to time. You might know the ones yourself, they sometimes have a red charity logo printed on the outside. They sometimes come round to your neighbourhood running a weekly collection, you know the kind of arrangement I'm sure. He would absolutely have stored them safely in the little wooden chest, the one with the blue and brass lamp on top, sensing that they would be useful to keep and that they would have their time one day, one good day, a special day.

You see, it certainly turns out that men are very good at keeping things, far better than women are, and particularly things that you can put other things in. A sort of Russian Doll idea I suppose. It all somehow just appeals to the creature that is a man, it brings a rare and deep connection to him in fact to be just plain excellent at what we may call ... storage. That would be things like wallets, a simple good pencil case was always a source of deep joy for him too, containers for his comprehensive collection of tools, glass jars ideally with their matching lid, ideally in gold but silver worked as well, many styles of bags, some made from linen, holdalls, ideally in dark green or black was fine too, cases, ones with lots of compartments and zips were just amazing to his practical mind, rare tubes of many sizes, some with a handy carry-strap attached firmly and most particularly just damned good, well-glued square boxes made from substantial cardboard. In brown ideally. He could fill a whole cupboard with those, and he was flexible on the brown. Yes, good boxes of many sizes in fact, because in this life you never know what you might need to put into a good box and for this reason the household would hear from time to time - "I can always find a home for this box, you never know when it might come in handy". Good man.

He soon found three of them safely put away. He climbed back up the stairs, with all three of them. If he hurried, he could just get down to the clothes bank in time for their six pm Friday evening collection.

Thirty eight shirts would soon be on someone else's back. And he could go back to being who he really was.

2. The Puppet that Pulled Back

He wasn't quite sure how to label it, what to call it if you like. Oh, he had a few ideas that were busy churning away still deep down inside his head but the final name label had not yet surfaced from his sub-conscious. It would do, definitely, and quite soon but not quite yet. The ninety percent of his mind that contemporary psychology books told him was his sub-conscious mind needed to work through its processes naturally and do what it did so well but it needed to do it at its own pace. He was absolutely certain that the label would appear at some point, like a bubble of air rising to the surface of a beautiful blue lagoon on a bright summer's day in the paradise of his amazing planet. For he knew that the subconscious can be a very powerful force that lives inside each and every one of us and that his was possibly even more creative and even more powerful than that of the next man or woman along. So he would let it churn away then, and do its cerebral stuff, rather like a spin dryer does and then suddenly before you know it the damp washing has now become nicely dried and can be put away into its proper place. Yes, he rather liked this particular notion, that the subconscious mind could be compared to the humble metallic tumble dryer that lives in so many people's kitchens and utility rooms and that it goes onto one of its many interminably slow drying programmes, yet it always gets its job done in the end and comes up with the goods, the dried goods in this case. Sorted!

You see he had heard this intriguing notion quite some time ago that we were being "played". He had read somewhere, probably in one of the many popular psychology books that he enjoyed reading continually, that what you might call the business of human existence on this quite exceptional planet that we call "Earth" was perhaps not quite what it seems, and that it had a few surprises up its biological sleeve, if you like. God no, wait a minute! That was not what it was saying at all! It was far more clear in its message than just that. What it was actually saying was that the business of human existence is in fact completely different to how it seems to us, in fact it could not be much more different. Yes, that was what "the notion" was saying all right. You see, we are not living here on a beautiful planet "hung in the blackness of space", a planet that is one of billions of planets in what we call the universe, through pure chance. For some this is one of the traditional views of the place of humans in this world.

The traditional views actually give you a choice, and say that we are either here by pure random chance or that if you believe in a God that we have been placed here and for a reason that only he knows. Think Chaos versus Evolution, chance versus intent, random versus planned. Whichever side of the intellectual fence you fall on, there is an option for you to take and go away and believe in for the rest of your natural life if you truly want to do that. Neat! Those who go for the religious view, well they head off to their church or to their mosque or to their synagogue and they spend the rest of their natural lives living in the company of like-minded people, genuflecting daily before their chosen God. Those who prefer the idea that life is purely a random thing well they head off to The Dog and Duck, or to The Queens Arms or to their local Starbucks to read, and to write and to discuss ideas of philosophy with companions. These are people who happily park outside a church but will rarely step inside one. Each to their own, we're all making it up as we go along each and every day, aren't we, winging it I do believe it's called?

Really? If we are being honest with ourselves, none of us really know what we're doing here do we, and if we're being honest with each other too. Just playing it by ear, taking each day as it comes, going with the flow, all that sort of thing, nice images of getting carried along rather pleasantly by the river that brings life.

So, let's go back to this curious notion that he had been exposed to in a book written by another human, which suggested that humans, and that's all humans, are being "played". Billions of us, and all at the same time. It suggested that we don't really exist in the way that we think we do, that our sense of reality is not quite "right" if we may use that word, and that the real truth is that there are other forces at work in our lives. And throughout the Universe. And it was suggesting that they are seriously damned big powerful forces too at that! It suggested very openly that in fact, and you really might need to be sitting down for this one, that we don't exist in the way they we think, not at all. Nope. Not a bit of it! Its hypothesis was that we are being fully controlled and right down to the point where even our perception of what's going on around us is being controlled too.

In short we are being tricked. We are all being deceived. Fooled would be a nice way of putting it. Manipulated would be another, and more like it. Controlled too, all the way down the line. At every junction as you travel on the highway of life. The notion you see suggested too that we are only around so long as the Great Divine continues to think about us, for we are nothing more than a fleeting thought in the mind of an unimaginably powerful Being (let's give her a capital B shall we?). So long as he/she/it/them continues to think about us and hold us in a thought then we may be allowed to continue to exist for an undetermined period of time. But the moment that the Great One starts thinking of something else and the thought of us is lost, well then so the light of our existence is extinguished. That quickly. In an instant. Bosh! That's the deal boys and girls. Take it or leave it. Brutal. In short, we are nothing more than characters in the computer game of a Being far higher and far more powerful than all of us put together. But this guy is seriously more powerful, okay, on a much higher level than any of us could ever be. We are being "played", we are in play each and every day and we are being played with. Hmmm, now that's quite a thought isn't it, that you and I are someone else's play thing? If it's true then it rather offers us a wholly different level of perspective on the business of life, don't you think? That's your life, and mine too.

He sipped his breakfast tea. The local Starbucks was moderately busy on that particular morning. Neither the church nor the mosque nor the synagogue was for him, although he knew where they all were and how parking outside them could be quite good most mornings, before seven. Disappointingly, none of the women taking tea in there though was very attractive to him on that particular morning, not to his discerning eyes anyway, and that was a shame. You see it was usually a place of great physical female beauty, where the fairer sex might be studied legitimately quite close up, but for some reason it wasn't happening, just not today. The Star in Starbucks was not shining very brightly on that morning. Pity. Great pity, it was one of the reasons that he kept going there, as opposed to Costa where the Ugly Factor was strangely far greater, and consistently so. So he had become a Starbucks guy then.

As he chewed this intriguing notion over, he realised that it was actually entirely comparable to the long standing Greek notion that we humans were down here on the surface of the planet and that far, far above us dwelled "The Great Gods".

It was really the same idea fundamentally. High up on Mount Olympus there lived Divine Entities who were far more powerful than we could ever imagine and who held our lives in their hands. They too played with the lives of we mere mortals as if in a giant and complex computer game. What they chose for us would surely come to pass and there was "Sweet FA" that we could do about it. Think of the powerful waves that come washing up onto a beach, think of the sun rising and falling each and every day relentlessly, and think of the dust that will gather in your home over time if you don't clean it, so too their divine wishes will soon become our mundane realty. Or so we think anyway, whatever "thinking" actually is. Perhaps we should replace "think" with the word "perceive" anyway, it's a more accurate reflection of what happens inside our mind, don't you think? We can only see for we never really know do we?

So, there you have it. That was the troubling notion that was going round inside his head. He had probably first bumped into it several human years ago but there must have been something about it that he liked deep down and that had appealed greatly to him for he had really not been able to shake it off fully. Like a coin that had fallen out of the pocket of a damp pair of blue jeans that were being dried in that same metallic tumble dryer, so the heavy coin rattled around inside noisily as the drum turned and you just knew that it was still in there. The noise you see was just too great for you to ignore.

As an idea of course it just seemed too stupid to be true, it seemed plainly absurd in fact, and it actually offered a very depressing view of the existence of the seven billion or so of us currently walking across the surface of this stupendous planet. Don't you think? If there really was no "After Life", and that it turns out that our existence is nothing more than the brief thought in the mind of a Great Being who is allowed to switch its thoughts whenever it chooses, then ouch! How crap is that? The word "temporary" comes to my mind to describe what you and I are doing here, but seriously temporary. Ephemeral. All She has to do is switch Her thinking and we get switched off, you and me. Bosh! That's the deal boys and girls. Nothing you can do to renegotiate the terms on this one I'm afraid. Done deal, switched off like exactly you do a light in your own house.

He ordered another cup of tea, and paid a ridiculous £2.80 for the privilege. How much profit must the faceless Starbucks Corporation be making he thought by charging him £2.80 for a cheap plastic cup (albeit with a lid), a tea bag and some hot water. About £2.50 was what he estimated, after all conceivable possible costs. That is of course, if he really even existed in the first place, and if there really was such a thing as a Starbucks coffee store and if the second paper cup of hot tea that he would soon be drinking really "existed" too. It certainly felt like he was inside a real Starbucks, and that the wooden round table and uncomfortable chair were real enough and that the smelly air conditioning system with the stench of bacteria that needed changing was real enough too. It really did smell seriously stale. And his tea felt and tasted good and it was pretty hot too. But, let's not forget that the notion said that if the Great Being wanted him to believe in all of those things because this was the thought that the Great Being had just thought then he would think all of those things, wouldn't he? If he wanted you to think that your Starbucks tea was a real thing and that it was hot, well then the taste would be there, right, and the temperature too? If he wanted you to think that the aircon was in need of a change then it would smell bad, right? If he wanted you to find the wooden chair uncomfortable then it would, right? Remember, we go where The Great Being thinks us to go, or had you forgotten that already good people?

Prepare to be switched off in an instant like a pot of Starbucks coffee. Bosh! That's the deal boys and girls. Like a light going out.

As He thinks, so we do, and so we exist. Or so we think. But who really knows, and what does this "knowing" word really mean anyway? Perception it would seem is indeed Everything then. The lenses through which you see the world around you are all powerful. The Great Being, the Great Divine, the Master Optician.

So, he just got on with his life, like you do, like we all do. Like you do because we have no choice and the world just keeps on turning. That's the deal boys and girls. We still have to eat food and drink drinks, we still have the regular bills to pay and we need to survive in the bankrupt capitalist times that we have created. Money is King. It isn't of course, it never will be, and it never could be, it will eventually get dethroned as a concept one wonderful, wonderful day but until then Money is the King on the Block. According to The Mail on Sunday anyway. And so we go to work, to earn cash, so that we can play the game. Perhaps we are being played in more ways than one? And as he immersed himself in the mundane business of daily life, so he would get sucked into the machine, and treated like all of the other perfect fat little sausages that came out of the other end. He was just a number, just another number on the employee payroll, yet another member of the human species that was really not special in any way different from the rest of them, that's the seven billion others that there appear to be. For those Accountants amongst you.

And yet, this one got what we might call "glimpses". He got glimpses if you like of someone behind the spotlight. That bright light that shone down on us every day, that light that gave us heat and meaning too, well it appeared to have someone or some thing that might been seen standing behind and operating it! And then he would get sucked back into the sausage machine of human routine and would be required to take part again in the daily grind that is life and he would very nearly forget the forbidden and terrifying glimpses that he had just got. It was as though his mind was being wiped regularly like we do to a laptop computer or to a mobile phone, and so you start all over again.

…. except that in his case, there was just a tiny little bit of memory that was left in his head. The faceless machine that washed our minds of all early memory wasn't quite as perfect as its maker perhaps thought it was. In short, it had missed a bit! Either that, or this man's mind was just a tad different from all of the others around him and the machine didn't wipe his memory completely clean like it was supposed to, not one hundred per cent clean. He would get those "Deja Vu" moments, like we all do I guess, and he too would sense that he had been in an identical situation before but without being able to say when exactly. Most of us have experienced those same moments in time at some point in our lives, haven't we? And they come and they soon go and we then even forget that we ever had them in the first place as we get pulled back into the daily grind of existing, of walking over, kneeling and worshipping at the Throne of King Money. I think that we are meant to forget too, and completely forget. The theory says that there is some kind of system at work that makes us forget. Like the God Amnesia draping his veil over us that makes us forget everything before. Global thought control would be about right as a description, or something like that anyway.

This one employee, number 118, seemed to have a vestige of memory that wasn't supposed to be there. It should have been wiped clean by the global thought control team but they had failed in his case. So he was fractionally different from all of the others, just ever so slightly so, a deviant, and a good one too! Perhaps technically by the Divine's standards he was a mutant or even a reject and therefore he should have been pulled from the production line to be recycled in some way. However it had come about, however he had been allowed to move down the production line, he now seemed to have just a tiny little bit of ability to keep hold of something that the Maker wanted to take back from him completely. For he could remember things better than his neighbour, and that made a huge difference.

Glimpses, terrifying glimpses.

But why? Why did that one thing make such a difference?

Because it made him able to put patterns together in his head. He could see design quietly working away behind the scenes. It let him develop a higher awareness of structure at work in the life of human beings. If you like, it let him get a sufficient number of glimpses of the terrible living creature that exists behind the bright spotlight that shines down on us each and every day and therefore to hang on to the notion that in the life of human beings perhaps all is not how it appears. Or all is not how we are meant to see it. By the way, others around him could have seen the creature moving around clumsily behind the light too if they had wanted to, all they needed to was to develop the same thirst for knowledge that he had developed and just to look, to see, and to notice it, but precious few of them did that.

Mindfulness, just a few drops from the bottle, that was all it took.

All they needed to do was to look up just a few more degrees and gain a perspective that was different to their normal daily one, but precious few of them did that. All that was needed was to make a decision to change a habit of a lifetime and to think differently today, just for one single day, but guess what, precious few of them did that. It did seem to him, human number 118, that amongst all of this huge, huge complexity there really were some stunning pieces of simplicity lying around and effectively staring back up at us in the face. Like huge pieces of bright and shiny glass, they were very definitely there for us to look at and bend down and even pick up with our hands, that's if we wanted to. All we had to do, was to choose to see and to choose actively to think differently and to choose to change our patterns of daily behaviour just very, very slightly, and yet, guess again, precious few of them did that. We are indeed creatures of habit, but then again maybe that's how we were made, how we came off the conveyer belt of life, one after the other, after the other, after the other... Maybe like a man-made motor car, we also come with built-in obsolescence, intellectual obsolescence in our case. Maybe we were not made able to see. No headlights then! Some cars just don't have a leather interior, or a sunroof or heated seats, perhaps some humans too are made with basic features only, entering the world with built-in intellectual obsolescence, with no internal SatNav if you like. Think high spec and low spec models, or something along those lines anyway.

That is how it was beginning to seem to him more and more, for he could not understand why other people around him just wouldn't look, see and notice. Perhaps they couldn't number 118, perhaps they just couldn't. Although he disliked the idea for so many reasons, perhaps he was one of the higher spec models, with just plain more features as part of the deal. He wasn't very comfortable with that idea, because it smacked of the traditional saying of "Pride before a Fall", the idea that if you indulge yourself and think that you're good at something that life soon has an irritating habit of tripping you up and showing you that you're really not that good at it, now are you?! However, the idea that he was perhaps a little "higher spec" did go some way to explaining why he saw what others around him didn't. They didn't know what they didn't know. At least he had got that first basic bit figured out. Like the goldfish that just swims round and round its bowl, it's happy. Relatively of course that is, until another slightly more clued up fish swims over to tell him the news that there is a whole new world out there. The other people seemed a little closer to the goldfish than he was perhaps. Slightly lower in their "Factory Specification" possibly?

Oh. Oh dear. Could people really come that limited? Was blindness of the mind really that common? That idea did take his mood down. You might think that it would buoy him up, to even dare to think that he was, potentially anyway, a cut above the rest, that he might be one of the higher spec models, but you see he was a humanist, a Corbynite, and he wanted his species to excel at some things, yet that was really not looking very likely. As a species it appeared to be firmly on the road to Mediocrity, and that was one seriously missed opportunity as he saw it. We could be doing so much better than this, so very much better. In this regard, he was a disappointed man.

Someone had once asked him at a very cheesy cocktail party if he believed in fate. It was cheesy in the literal sense, for there were vast plates of cubes of cheese on cocktail sticks with chunks of pineapple on offer for all to take. The people there had been dressed in a very cheesy way too, it was all really rather like a cheesy dream from the planet Gorgonzola. If a well-dressed butler had walked into the picture carrying a huge tray of Ferrero Rocher chocolates in their characteristic gold foil wrappers he would not have been in the least bit surprised, that's just how cheesy the whole cheesy evening was. All it would then take would be for a middle-aged man in a white polo neck jumper and a red cardigan to arrive carrying a purple box of Milk Tray chocolates too with the 007 theme music playing in the background and the cheesiness would have been perfectly complete. Cheese Factor number 10, that's the maximum legally allowable I think! Anyway, back to the cheesy party, there he was one winter's evening near Christmas time drinking cheesy fizzy wine, and eating cheesy snacks, talking to this cheesy young lady wearing a little black dress that was impossibly tight on her, and then she asked him the question:

"So tell me then, do you believe in Fate?"

He wasn't usually short for words, number 118, but on this occasion he had to think hard about his answer. Like most people he doesn't like silence in the conversation and so he did that thing that many people do when they need to buy themselves just a smidgeon more of time in order to think of an answer and he repeated her question back to her, repeating it twice actually:

"Do I believe in Fate...? Do I believe in Fate?"

Steadily, an answer began to form in his mind. He went on to say to the cheesy woman that he believed in the impact of circumstance on a person's life. Was that the same as Fate, he wasn't sure. But a child born let's say in a remote village in the middle of Africa was almost certainly on a path in his or her life that they were unlikely to be able to change. Again, they didn't know what they didn't know. What you grow up with as "normal" remains normal to you. A young man born into an affluent family on the East Coast of The United States whose father has made a personal fortune in the world of Financial Asset Management, whatever that may be, is also likely to be on a path in his life already. Likewise, a beautiful young lady who gets spotted at an early age and who goes onto to be a famous model and an actress and a celebrity author, well she too is probably also a victim of circumstance, but in a different way to the African child. Yes, he thought aloud to his cheesy companion, if that is how we define Fate then yes he replied to her, then he believed in Fate. A man in a white polo neck jumper walked past them both, while Jingle Bells sung by the Cardiff Male Voice Choir played in the background. The Black Forest Gateau would shortly be served. Followed by yet more cheese.

Fate in that sense of the word, in the sense that the set of circumstances that you are born into shapes your life, yes he thought he believed in that definition of fate. Your parents, their way of life, their religious beliefs, their drinking and eating habits, their own backgrounds, your job, your attitude to food and to exercise, your neighbourhood, your partners in life, your siblings, your school days, all of these things he considered to play a significant role in shaping the path that your life was likely to follow. He thought that he could remember reading a book some time back where the label "Environmental Determinism" had been used. Nature or Nurture? Well, the Environmental Determinists out there thought that Nurture played a big part. What happened to you after coming into the world was where it was for them. Others thought that your life was shaped heavily by our nine months in our mother's womb. Ah yes, the power of gestation he commented to Lady Cheese, at which point an expression of not inconsiderable confusion quickly splashed over her face. What he was very clear on was that the decisions that we make in our lives have a major effect on how things turn out, things like our partners, our careers, our lifestyles, our politics and our religious choices too perhaps. And even cheese too, probably. If we are indeed born with a blank sheet of paper to write on throughout our life, then our decisions probably write the larger words on that paper, more so than almost anything else does. Yes, he seemed quietly confident about this last point. A moment of inspiration then rushed into his head.

"After all, like the wise man once said, you're born, you suffer and then you die!"

he said to her provocatively, and in a very bold voice, genuinely inviting her to respond in some way. He really wanted her to disagree with him, or to agree, or at the very least to react in some way. Please? Pretty please...But no, a reaction there was not. The intellectual cupboard was apparently bare. The wave of confusion washed over her face again, this time the wave was a little deeper. A strong English Cheddar clearly slowed down the mind, in her case anyway. The absurdly tight black dress probably didn't help either. It was time to move on he thought, and find another conversational partner. Time to find the Black Forest gateau too he reckoned. Mind, she did have great tits, really great.

He had experienced good times in his life, and then like most other people they would merge into times that were less good, perhaps even bad. Life's like that, isn't it? It's rarely consistent in how it treats us, right? The thing that he had been plain slow to learn was that we humans have these things called "Expectations". They reside somewhere inside us, perhaps in our mind, perhaps in our heart, and they are simply huge. Huge do you hear me? Yet, and here is the really extraordinary thing, despite their size, you can't see them! How weird is that? Most people don't really see them by the way, at least not regularly or even very clearly. They are enormous, they are huge, they may be as big as a mountain, and they drive what we think "should" happen in our lives. However, despite all of this, we never share them, or talk about them or even acknowledge them. At least, very, very rarely. And that's not good don't you think? 118 had been slow to realise this in his own life, but being the higher spec model at least he had begun to see it. The goldfish swimming round in circle after circle around him wouldn't be able to see it, but at least as he was entering his forties, he could begin to sense the power of expectation just a little more than everyone else could. He had the beginning of an awareness of just how big a force expectation can be in a person's life. He had begun to work that out for himself, - well done him! A little bit of progress then in his modest life. He had also worked out that the sooner that we can either modify our expectations or maybe even ditch them completely then so much the better! Whence they came, he knew not. But what he was very clear on was that they are very real, that they aren't going to go away any time soon and that they need to be taken out and allowed to see the sun more often than happens generally. Keeping them tightly under wraps and never discussing them is potentially quite dangerous. Whoever the great Puppeteer is above us, pulling our strings whenever he wants to, he knows about the power of expectations in our lives all right. In fact he probably had them built in to his puppets in the first place. Clever idea that one, particularly wiring up a good string to bring them into action whenever he wants to with a sharp tug. Damned clever idea, for him anyway!

And we are powerless to change a thing. That's the deal boys and girls. Like the wise man said, "You're born, you suffer, and you die". The phrase that cheesy lady did not much appreciate.

He recently heard a scientist being interviewed on a television documentary about the rise of life on this planet. The scientist had said a very interesting thing that had stayed in his head many months later. The scientist had simply asked this question:

"We know that a human being is a combination of hydrogen and carbon molecules. So how is it that a bunch of molecules can get to a point where they ask where they came from?!"

He thought that was a very fine question, a really very fine question indeed. He liked the fact that in one single question it brought both science and philosophy together, for that appealed to him greatly. Perhaps they were not natural bed fellows, Mr Science and Miss Philosophy. What it did highlight too of course is that we do live a very physical life. We are indeed made of carbon and hydrogen and weren't we supposed to be something like ninety per cent water? Was that right? The sheer physicality of the human experience is all too easy to overlook, but ask the emergency medical team working in the Accident and Emergency ward of any large National Health Service hospital if they understand the physical reality of flesh and bone, and blood too, and they will of course be very aware of that side of our lives. Especially on the night of a full moon, really. We appear to be entirely physical entities he would often reflect over his £2.80 cup of bland tea, always served in a tall paper cup, up in his local Starbucks. Even if we are Consciousness in essence, we still have a physical frame. Entities that are entirely subject to the laws of physics, physical laws that dictate to us that we must put food and water into our bodies ideally two or three times a day, that we must sleep for at least six hours in a day, that if you stay out in the sun for too long that your skin will actually burn, although you may not realise this at the time, that the sea will come into the shore and then recede again twice daily as a result of the magnetic influence of the Moon on the sea, laws that mean when you drop a slice of good proper wholemeal toast with Frank Cooper Oxford marmalade on the top that it may well land butter side down, and it generally does.

For these are powerful laws indeed and ones that we are utterly powerless to change. That's the deal boys and girls. Your car just will definitely become dirty over time, even if it sits on your driveway without being driven anywhere for a whole week. The dirt just does come along. Statistically the local flock of pterodactyls will dump over your nice clean car too during that same week. One day when walking about you just may find that something unpleasant, normally in a light or dark brown colour, may have attached itself to the underside of your nice new shoes - what a pain, particularly if you're just about to climb into your car. One day you will begin to sense the not unfamiliar pain of toothache and it will likely build up to the point where you need to get a man in a white jacket to poke cold metal tools around your warm mouth in order to relieve the discomfort. You might also find a lump in your groin, or on your breast one worrisome day, and feel the need to book an urgent appointment with your local family doctor to get their professional opinion on what it is, and what treatment may or may not be needed in order to make the lump go away. To get there, you will need to leave your little house with its green front door, lock that same door from the outside, and climb into your new electric hatchback car, and drive down there, making sure that there is none of that nasty brown stuff attached to the underside of your nice new shoes too this time. That would not be good, as that would be the very least of your worries on that particular morning.

Meanwhile, there is an asteroid of significant proportions heading towards your planet at unimaginably high speed that is due to slam into the Earth in fourteen and half months' time, on a Tuesday morning actually, at about 06.45 am just as you're getting up to go to catch your regular train to work. The scientists and the US Government know all about it as they have been tracking it for over two long months now, but we don't, you don't, because you don't need to at this point in time. You will be informed at "the appropriate time", whatever that phrase means. It's a visitor from deep space that is made of dirt and mud and rock and snow and ice, and this is the raw physicality of a monstrous thing from deep space slamming into the physicality of fragile little planet Earth.

Meanwhile, back at the ranch, you have very little food in your house with its little green front door and so your electric hatchback car is needed yet again to take you down to your local supermarket to go and bring bags of fresh food home back into your house. Again you must lock that door as you leave your home with a cold metal key. That food has been grown in fields of dark and cold black earth, or in moist manmade clinical greenhouses, the silver scaly fish that you have bought in the supermarket have all been pulled violently from out of the vast blue oceans with a long wire net pulled behind a rust-clad metal boat that still somehow stays afloat on the turbulent seas. The amazing uniformly crisp green apples of an English farm have been manually pulled from a heavily cultivated tree and placed into a box made of wood from another type of tree and that box placed with hundreds of others to be loaded into a grubby diesel truck and transported safely along grey tarmac motorways to a shiny glass national distribution centre to be washed with good water and prepared to European standard number 1234 and labelled with recycled paper before being driven in the early hours of the morning sixty four miles down a second motorway to your local supermarket to be placed, again by a human hand, onto a wooden shelf at just the right height for you to reach out and grasp them and place them into your silver metallic supermarket trolley, a trolley whose handle is certainly riddled with Corona germs from so many other people's hands.

You then pay for them with some heavy metal gold coins, getting a paper receipt, and you drive them home in that electric hatchback car again and having opened your front door once more you place them, again by hand, into a fruit bowl inside your warm home, varnished in green and blue made of heavy clay dug out of the land by some sweaty dark-haired olive-skinned men born somewhere in a place named Tuscany, in a country known as Italy. Where they await their fruity fate... meanwhile your nice expensive white work shirts need to have a good wash and so you place them into your metal washing machine, now filled with fragrant Lily washing powder, Ocean Breeze version, and set to the hot "Whites Only" washing setting, so that the dirt from the previous day's toil can be physically taken out of the cotton shirt material by the mechanical process provided by a machine. Shirts that will soon be placed into your shiny new tumble dryer where the excess and unwanted water will be physically spun out of the shirts, by a centrifugal process.

We do indeed live a very physical existence most of the time. We are dependent on things around us, and perhaps above us too. The Grand Puppeteer is always at his work high above the stage... and this was a man who would get glimpses of this happening, glimpses of the monster behind the bright light that he was not supposed to be able to see, ever. There appeared to this one individual man to be a set of laws at work, laws that delivered light and air and gravity and water and tea and coffee, and bright red tomatoes and crisp green apples, laws that might give a human a matter of hours of life on this planet or as long as one hundred years of life. There would be lots in between. Laws that said that life could come about if your planet was in "The Goldilocks Zone" and was at just the right distance from the burning heat of a nearby star. Laws that offered more planets in the known universe than there were thought to be grains of sand on our one planet, laws that appeared to say that the universe was expanding continually, but just what was where it was expanding into? How could there be nothing and then there was something? These were surely concepts that little old us were not even supposed to know about, yet alone comprehend. Everything is relative, relative to where you're starting out from. The little green guys and the scary tall reptilian aliens and the nine foot tall blonde Scandic Beings were aliens to us but weren't we exactly the same to them? Depends on your starting point, where you're coming from, what glasses you're wearing and the prism through which you see. Right?

Sometimes he would marvel at the laws that he thought he could identify at work all around him. They were literally marvellous. He was in awe of them, whoever their author was, boy did he know what he was doing. We were the puppets and he was the Grand Puppeteer, and that boys and girls was the deal. Go with it, do not question it, just go with the celestial flow. Drink from The Milky Way and ask for no more for you will be given no more. Be happy that you have been granted an existence, for it will be taken away from you when you least expect it. When you least expect it! There are viruses that can be applied …

Then on other days that awe would be replaced with anger, as he saw the world and his place in it quite differently. We were being played, for sure, we were someone else's play thing, and he did not like that one bit! We were being used, in someone else's game. Why didn't everybody else see it? On days like this he would lose all respect for the Grand Master, his own creator, and that was probably not a good idea, not a very good idea at all. For it was his game and if he switched thoughts then like a light, we get turned off. That is how the game works, the rules are only too clear. This was manipulation on a planetary scale, manipulation of an entire species by someone or something who was very much in charge.

The Boss, the Big Cheese, the whole enchilada, God, the Big Man, the guy up Top, Head Honcho, the Manager, The Great Divine, The Almighty, the Powerful one, The Special One, the Omnipotent, the Great Deity, The Great Gods, The White Light, The Guvnor... the Grand Puppeteer who pulled strings day in and day out, our strings, yours and mine.

He had had enough. It was a bright sunny day but he was worrying about so many things in his life. He was overcome for the first time in his terrestrial life with a deep fear that he could not deal with all of it. He was consumed with the Fear, and his normal controlled behaviours had left him that morning. He threw his paperwork to the floor, bank statements flying off the table, the grim letter from the hospital too, his paper cup of Starbucks bland £ 2.80 tea sent flying, and he burst through the French doors and out into the sun.

"I know you're there, hiding behind the sun! Show yourself, come on! Show yourself! If you're so clever, step out from behind the light and let me see you head on. Just for once! I know that you're there, and you know I know, so have the balls to appear! Have the balls!" he shouted aloud.

The sun was too bright for him to stare into for more than half of one second. He felt a pain in his chest, and he shouted again:

"Show yourself, Mr Puppeteer. Come on, put the wooden frame down just for a moment and let me know what I know about you! Come on, show yourself! Coward! Coward! Coward! Coward! Coward!" he shouted still louder.

The pain in his chest intensified still further, and he was now not able to stand in the sunlight. He fell to the floor, clutching his chest in life-sapping pain. The Grand Puppeteer had not shown himself as asked to then, he had not stepped out from behind the light this time, and he had not put the wooden frame and strings down for just a few moments as the puppet who had pulled back had asked of his Maker, busy at work high, high above the stage.

And yet, in pulling that one last string, The Grand Master had in fact confirmed His very existence from up high, high above. The Master Puppeteer never, but never, puts down the frame of strings, not for any man or woman, and he alone had the power to decide that this puppet would very soon dance no more.

3. Martin's New Year

Martin was actually quite a busy man. He was a very busy man in fact. Well you would be wouldn't you, running a busy high-profile newsagents shop on a busy high street. like his often was? This was a man who was fully committed to his job, for he worked hard at it and he could tell his friends truthfully that he enjoyed this kind of work most of the time. As a line in honest, legal and morally upright work, it had been good to him over the years and he in turn had been good to the shop too. They were very good partners it seemed to him.

One evening towards the end of December 2018, after a very busy day of selling even more special glitzy Christmas chocolate selection boxes than he had sold the day before, all available by the way at reduced prices by now, Martin personally shut up his shop exactly on time at 6 pm and went up the narrow "39 steps" as he called them to his clean flat above. There were actually twenty three stairs in truth, but he pretended there were more as he had read that famous book. There were now very few customers around anyway at that time on a bitterly cold winter's evening, and so he decided that it was time to "call it a day" as they say at the end of a long old day in the retail trade, and also that he could relax just a little for the evening ahead.

Sandra his lovely girlfriend would be home later about 9.00pm that evening, also after another long day working in the local NHS hospital. She was a very good nurse, highly qualified in several important areas, with an excellent bedside manner and many patients had complimented her recently on how good she was with her hands. Martin really liked that in a nurse. It was a very desirable quality for him.

Martin made a good winter pot of tea, and sat down at their modest IKEA table to write down a few ideas that had been going round and round his head throughout his busy day ever since his early 5.30 am start. After twelve hours stood standing on his poor old feet he reckoned that he certainly deserved a brew and the chance to put his feet up, literally, but he also really wanted to make some good notes while he could remember those ideas he had been having. He loosened his Jermyn Street striped silk tie, just a little. As he waited for the Waitrose Essentials breakfast tea to mix with the hot water in the traditional red teapot just a minute or two longer, he found a notepad and an HB pencil and sat down at the little table to start writing down those important things from earlier in his day. In his line of business of course there was never any shortage of pencils and paper, or of chocolate selections, of sellotape or of shall we say "interesting" magazines either for that matter.

His favourite joke down the Queens Head on a Thursday evening was to say that you could even read some of the magazines too, if you really wanted to! How the public bar laughed aloud as they supped!

"Martin, what are you like, eh?!" Quite the funniest newsagent around for miles …

Actually, the accurate truth was that Martin was a particularly well read man. He didn't have a university education, you see his academic studying had stopped at eighteen when to his considerable satisfaction he got three reasonable A levels, and he then moved into the dizzy world of office work. It was office work high up on the third floor too, only the best for Martin! However, here was a decent enough man of really very good intelligence who had deliberately bettered himself in life by reading a good old-fashioned newspaper from cover to cover pretty well every day of his working life, year in year out. He was street-wise was Martin and people sought out his views on a topic, from time to time. He liked a good quality silk tie as well, never a cheap polyester tie for this man, oh no! The public bar knew that if Martin hadn't read about it in one of the papers that day, then it was probably not big news or even worth noting in the first place! He also took good time to buy unusual magazines and books from his wholesaler to sell on in his shop, for he relished solid books on politics, history and philosophy in particular. Yes, this was a bright, energetic and well informed man, running his own successful local business, a man who had views on many aspects of life that were fuelled both through personal experience but also by a plain good old-fashioned grasp of the facts.

Many of the books and magazines available today on the shelves in his newsagents shop would typically spend their first few days in his flat above the shop being studied and read by him personally with great care. He would turn the pages very carefully wearing one of those free plastic gloves you get at petrol stations on his left hand, so that they could be put on the shelves in the shop below just a few days later for sale to his customers, still in pristine condition. Late one Thursday evening in September, he had got so utterly carried away with a glossy hardback guide to Morality and Ethics, (retailing for just £4.99), that he had started to write some personal notes in black ink at the side of many of the pages. How very careless and unusual this was of this normally very precise man. One morning the local estate agent had brought the same book back to the shop complaining that there was someone's strange scribbling in his brand new book that he had bought from Martin only a few days before, and could he swap the book for a new one or get a refund please? It was all rather grubby you see, and if he could get a clean copy that would be helpful.

"Estate agent challenges Newsagent" would be the headline here of course, what an epic battle that would be!

"Gosh!" said Martin, "I wonder how on this earth that could have happened?" He gave his customer another clean copy from a box to the left of the till immediately, apologized for the inconvenience that he had gone through and said to him "Oh, I think you'll enjoy chapter seven by the way, it's really very good, it pulls the whole book together very nicely!" Sadly, his customer left the shop that morning really none the wiser on the vital topic of Morality and Ethics, useful in the world of property one would imagine, none the wiser at that particular point in time anyway, perhaps later. People would do well generally to listen to modest Martin. He was an informed individual even though he ran a single and modest enough Newsagents.

So that December evening, he felt a strong need to record some of the ideas that had begun to occur to him for what seemed like no particular reason earlier in his working day. He had this notion that the ideas had most probably been started off in his head by an article that he had read first thing that day as he was sorting through the morning papers.

He couldn't recall which newspaper it was in, but he had briefly read a short piece, sipping his traditional breakfast tea of course, about how the end of a year and the start of a new one gave us all:

"A unique opportunity to look back at the old year and decide what to do differently in the next one!"

Martin already knew from reading seven books on ancient civilizations that after all the month of January was named after the two-faced Roman god Janus who both looked back at the outgoing year as well as looking forward to the new one coming in. That idea in the newspaper article had appealed to him considerably, and it had really built a strangely firm connection in his head in an instant, although he had not realized this at the time. It seemed entirely logical as an idea, very practical too. It had had kicked off quite an energetic bit of thinking in Martin's head that day, as he sorted through all of the newspapers, as he sold dozens of pints of Cravendale semi-skimmed and full cream milk to all manner of people walking into his shop and as he wished all of his regular Customers good luck with their regular Euro Millions and lottery ticket purchases. Another busy morning.

He was not normally that cerebral, but the planets really appeared to have aligned that day or something like it anyway, because he kept getting these new ideas popping up in his head as he was serving Customers in his bright little shop, and they just kept on coming regularly throughout the day. 2018 had not been a bad year, quite a good year in fact from the business point of view, so he didn't think that they were born out of dissatisfaction with the outgoing year. He thought it was more likely that he was in a positive frame of mind about the new year of 2019. Yes, that was it, he had concluded, he was really looking forward to this next year, and that was why he was coming up with these exciting new ideas for improvement, exactly like the newspaper article had suggested that we all might.

It was only a few weeks since the lovely and dexterous nurse Sandra had moved in with him, so he was very excited about that and perhaps this in itself provided another reason to look forward to their first full year together. He smiled a little at the effect of thinking positively, loosened his quality striped silk tie still further, and poured himself a fresh brew. He drank Waitrose Essentials tea always, and always too with full cream milk. Just the best.

He had brought some milk upstairs with him from the shop, Cravendale milk of course that was "So good the cows want it back" as they said in their Marketing. For this was something else that he was never short of in his line of work, milk. When drinking tea he simply preferred full cream. So did Sandra come to think of it, clever girl, a slight smug smile slowly appearing across the naughty newsagent's lips.

His first word on the notepad written in dark grey pencil was just the date "2019", followed on the line underneath by the words "What we can do differently". He took a Helix aluminium twelve inch ruler and underlined both with great precision. He poured the full cream milk into his brown mug of tea, and said aloud to himself:

"Now, what to do differently next year....2019... I wonder...little old me, and all of us too?"

An idea came back quickly from the early morning paper sorting, and so he wrote it down.

1. Pick up litter every time you see some, even if it's not yours.

Yes, he liked that idea. Cool start. He was always finding litter around his shop and out on the high street as well, and he really disliked that. Leaving any kind of litter behind was not very considerate to other people first of all, and from the point of view of the reputation of his business as a local newsagent, it looked really bad, like he was supplying all of the litter material for the entire town from his one shop! He actually wasn't. Most of it seemed to come from the fast food outlets and cafes up the road, for you could see the Subway and Costa Coffee logos on it very clearly if you looked carefully enough, and not one of the ubiquitous plastic bags on the ground had come from his shop. Instead they carried the words "Tesco" in blue and "Sainsburys" in orange and "Morrisons" in bright yellow on them, for all to see. The polystyrene coffee cups that blew about in the wind all seemed to come from Costa Coffee a few shops down the High Street, and the small slips of white paper blowing around were generally the discarded paper slips from the Lloyds and Barclays cash machines further up the street. He had picked up one such cash slip off the floor one morning that he saw laying just outside his shop door as he was walking into work from a long hard night at Sandra's maisonette. He was amazed to the see the figure of £12,234.90 pence that was the current balance in the account. Lucky them, he thought, I only have £14,500 in my single savings account, let alone in a current account! The only other person who seemed to be as tidy and as professional as him was the young Asian lady selling the Big Issue on the corner of the office building that was next to his shop. He simply admired her good manners, and how she always greeted everyone with "Good Morning, Big Issue?" or "Good afternoon, Big Issue?" He always smiled at her, and she back to him, and in the recent cold weather he had taken some hot tea out to her one morning. You know the brand of tea by now. She had appreciated that greatly, and they smiled at each other for quite some time, their eyes lingering on each other's intelligent face. He had never mentioned this moment of connection to Sandra. He would offer her some hot tea again another time he had determined, perhaps a chocolate hobnob too, particularly on a very cold day.

The picking up litter idea was a good one he thought. "Do the math", as he had read in The Economist magazine they say in the US - if one million people picked up a piece of litter in this country every day, that would be at least five or six million less pieces of rubbish on the streets each working week and that meant a lot more material going into the re-cycling process too. That must surely be a good thing, he concluded.

Simple but effective! Yes, that was Martin all over.

Next on the list from his busy cerebral morning's work....

2. *Would all dog owners ensure this new year that their pet's mess is cleared up!*

No need to explain why we all benefited from this, right? This was an entirely reasonable request, thought the Newsagent.

Number three…

3. *We must all show courtesy to each other on the roads this year, let's start today!*

He was on a roll now. Number four read like this:

4. *Throw away less food each week, and aim to plan your meals better in 2019.*

That last idea seemed to come from the food rubbish specifically that he saw the fellow high street shops throwing out each day, and it worried him. Yes, that one definitely needed to be on the list for 2019, for sure.

Next ...

5. *We are all citizens of the same world, we all come into the shop of life! Let's show greater tolerance to each other in 2019 and to each other's ideas, whether these be religious, political or racial. Whatever.*

    Good, he felt that needed to be up near the top of the list, certainly in the first half dozen ideas.

The rest of his list included the following intentions:

6. *Don't shout at anyone, ever, and learn to listen more. Remember the "two ears and one mouth" idea, and use them in that proportion in this new year.*

He had heard someone shouting recently in the local Butcher's shop and it had stayed in his head. It was such a poor way to communicate after all, particularly over a few pork chops and some chicken thighs, so that was probably where that one came from.

And still more ideas came …

7. *I shall apply "The one minute rule" - this says that whenever you bump into someone, you should always give them at least one minute of your time, maybe more, no matter where you are going to. No-one is so busy that they can't do that, right?*

He liked this idea because it made sure that decent conversations were had and that those important little chats with his regular Customers in his shop were not rushed. As had happened a few times recently when it just got too busy.

8. *When did I last go and say hello to my neighbours?*

Yes, this was a good thing to plan to do too. He would go and see those two nice Danish girls who had moved into the flat next door. They seemed very friendly when they had come in the shop.

9. *Read more! The world has completely forgotten how important it is to read books - oh and join a book club too in 2019, they're great fun! Yes, I'll do that too.*

That would probably be easy since he loved reading papers and magazines all of the time. This next one was not his own idea, it had come from a copy of "Psychology" magazine, the April edition in fact.

10. *Treat every person that you meet with "Unconditional Positive Regard".*

He liked it and he thought that it mattered to include it on his list. The next logical step from this was to extend that same approach from humans to animals.

11. *Be kind to all animals, after all they share this planet with us remember. You could start by eating less of them - that really might be a nice place to start! I'm sure they would appreciate us doing that this year don't you?*

So this would be the year then when he finally went Pescatarian then! Good, this excited him. This was all now beginning to feel like a really good list of things to work on. He had planned on a maximum of ten things but the ideas kept coming.

So, what else …?

This next one was something that he had been thinking about for quite some time. He had nearly put it into operation last year but somehow he had got distracted.

> 12. I shall listen to a minimum of five minutes of classical music each and every day. It has the power to move your soul, like no other, so they say. A bit of soul moving is what this world needs more of.

Yes, that would be a very enjoyable one too. And this next one he thought was probably influenced by another edition some time back of the "Psychologies" magazine, although he was unable to remember which month exactly:

> 13. Have "Courageous Conversations" when you know inside that you need to have them. Those conversations that we know need having and which make things so much better if you have them soon and in a friendly, safe way. Try it this year, what have you got to lose?

The humble Martin was away by now, "on a roll" as they say, with all of the morning's thoughts and more flooding into his ambitious mind. All of those years of reading through early morning newspaper articles, of browsing book lists and of studying all of those unusual magazines and books that he had picked out for sale in his humble little shop, were giving rise to some seriously good ideas now.

On he went...

> 14. Meditate several times a week, it can produce simply amazing results. Try it, like the brave conversations above, what have you got to lose?

He already did something similar, but this would definitely be a good thing to start, he felt sure about that. And now his mind moved to bigger things in society and to one of the things that he thought was most of need of a damned good fix! Politics.

> 15. The system of politics in this country of ours need to change, and in the world too come to think of it. The recent MPs' expenses scandal was just one indication of that, but ours is a deeply flawed system that caters too easily to the egos of the party leaders and not to the true needs of the electorate who voted them into office in the first place! Let's replace the confrontation in politics with something called Integrity. But not with the existing players, we need new leaders and visionaries. So he would write to his local MP asking for a face to face meeting, to discuss this further.
>
> He poured some more tea, and sensed that his mind was slowing slightly now. Perhaps he had come to the end of his list for the evening. Just then however, as full cream milk was being poured into his mug, another idea from the busy morning in his shop rushed back into Martin's head. It had first occurred to him as he had shaken hands for the twenty sixth time that day with Customers wishing him all the best for

the New Year. It was what he liked to classify as a really modest and "low level idea" but it seemed to merit its place on the list for 2019.

16. *"After this winter's Norovirus outbreak (affecting over one million people according to The Times newpaper,) we would all do well to carry around with us a small bottle of antiseptic hand wash – this was a simple but potentially hugely effective habit for you and your family/friends/acquaintances to adopt." Yes, a little bottle of antiseptic handwash was a really sensible idea, and he would now do that as a matter of course.*

By now, Martin was really slowing down and so he took the time to boil his silver kettle and then pour himself some more tea. In went the full cream white milk again, but never sugar. He was looking forward to hearing nurse Sandra coming through the back door soon, her navy blue uniform swishing as she walked up the thirty nine steps. Now it was getting harder to remember all of the good thoughts from the morning.

Several cups of safely-made tea later and he was done. Brain had stopped working! Martin began to think how he could take this list of public New Year resolutions and do something really valuable with it. He thought about asking to have it published in the local "Citizen" newspaper and that was certainly a good idea, but the trouble with it was that unless people saw his article and deliberately cut it out to stick it up somewhere, then its impact was lost after just one week. "Today's newspaper is tomorrow's fish and chip wrapper!" as a wise fish and chip shop owner in Bolton had once remarked so well! His next idea was to produce some easy and cheap photocopies of his list of resolutions and just hand them out to his regular customers, asking them to do the same with their friends and work colleagues. That way their effect might be easily multiplied. He liked this idea too but he worried that it was not entirely appropriate for him to thrust his ideas on a sheet of A4 paper into their hands when they had only come into the shop to buy their morning paper or some cigarettes, and so early in the morning. Hmmm, another route to market was required.

Just then, the very attractive Sandra had entered the building, and her lovely professional legs had indeed started to take her up the now famous "39 steps" to their first floor flat.

"Hello entrepreneurial Newsagent man, how's your day been?" she asked, placing her stylish fake Armani bag on the sideboard.

"Oh you know, the usual thing, another busy day keeping the economy going, someone has to!" he replied.

"And you, has Sister Sandra been saving lives again then today, has she?"

"Of course, what else ever happens?" she replied, sounding half serious too.

"They have been talking about a really big epidemic coming our way this Winter, much bigger than the normal Winter Flu one we have. Better start buying little bottles of hand gel if I were you. They should sell very well, from what we're being told at work!"

He smiled at her and nodded in agreement. She was a clever girl was his Sandra.

"You know, it's the start of a new year and I was thinking that you really ought to re-arrange all of those for sale notices and scrappy bits of paper you have in the shop window too, it all looks terribly messy. It's worse than the nurse's desk on our ward!"

And there in a delicious moment was his next idea, courtesy of the gorgeous medical professional lady. He would re-arrange the shop window like Sandra had just suggested, that did definitely need doing at some point anyway. She was right about so many things was his "nursey friend" and this was a very good time for her to be right. Sandra slipped off her blue uniform and went to run a bath, a reduced bottle of Radox "Ocean Blue" bath wash taken from the shop below clutched firmly in her warm right hand.

The next evening Martin put his idea into practice and after he had closed the busy shop at 6.01 pm, he got to work on his new shop window. He left the shop lights on full, locked the door with all four locks fully engaged, and pulled the summer blinds right down to the bottom of the white rectangular windows, to ensure his privacy. The colourful blinds had been provided to him free of charge courtesy of a well-known national manufacturer of ice-cream they and carried photos of the largest Solero ice-cream ever seen in Berkshire! Sandra enjoyed getting her lips round a good Solero too he had suddenly remembered, a satisfied smile lingering on his tired face. He wanted his shop window to look good the next morning, to provide a more cared for appearance than it had been doing recently and to just look a little fresher. What he was after was "visual impact"! He had read that term in a "Good Guide to Marketing" paperback one evening so that was what he would set out to achieve. Down came the local "for sale" notices advertising things like children's bicycles, unwanted washing machines and a tumble dryer, down came the "services" cards advertising the services of "a man with a van who can" and people who could do your ironing immaculately, change the brakes on your car at your convenience, or come round to your garden "to trim your bush".

The last to come down was his very own Christmas red and white advert price card that read "£1.45 per week, £5.20 for the whole month and £54 to advertise for a whole year". He would use that card again when the window was complete and so that was laid down carefully on top of the January edition of House and Garden, for later on you understand. As he was working away, his design skills started rising from within like they had never needed to before. He found a pack of colourful stickers that had fallen down behind one of the blinds. He had no idea how it got there but an exciting idea came into his mind in a flash. Why not make his New Year resolutions the centre piece of the newsagent's shop window? There would still be plenty of room for all of the Customers' colourful "For Sale" and "Wanted" notices etc. but if he could arrange things in the way that had just come into his newsprint-stained mind that might look very good and have the impact that he wanted.

It might also cause a little bit of a "stir" locally in the village which he was up for, and that wouldn't do his modest little goldmine too much harm either he concluded.

Two hours and three tea-breaks later, the job was done. There was a Mars bar, large size, eaten in there somewhere too. After all "A Mars a day helps you work, rest and play!", not forgetting either that "A Milky way is the sweet you can eat between meals without running your appetite!".

Life must be just so full of temptation of the sweet kind for a newsagent, don't you think?

Martin stepped back from his work and yes he rather liked what he saw. Good job, he thought. To the left of the window as he looked out, were the previous "For sale" notices. To the right could be found the "Wanted" cards and at the bottom were lots of colourful product stickers that the chocolate and ice cream manufacturers asked him to keep in his shop window, just to help to advertise their products.

He was fine with that. And sitting proudly therefore in the middle, and this time facing outwards into the shop, was his single poster of hand-written new year resolutions that he had drawn up that same night with a green marker pen. He had once read in a small hardback book you see on the topic of spirituality, (available at all good bookshops and newsagents like Martin's for just £5.99), that green was the colour that best symbolized new growth and personal development for you and so green seemed to be the natural choice of colour to write the new and exciting ideas down in. The large card looked good and could be seen quite easily by his customers queuing up at the till. Martin the professional stationer knew well which was the right stiffness of card to use for this job, but there was an important clever little twist too. For sheets of circular stickers were placed to the left of the main card in a little plastic wallet with an arrow advertising this:

"Place your Free Vote here!?"

He was only asking his Customers to vote with a colourful sticker for the New Year resolution for 2019 that they most wanted to come true! How innovative could this man be? Extraordinary!

"Wow Martin, what are you like?!" Pushing that envelope again are you? What a novel idea, clever little newsagent you. Not just selling the news but making it too!

He finished his tea with full cream milk and called his buddy down into the shop to see his work, the now well-oiled Sandra sliding down the stairs in her lilac negligee and matching mules. She was very impressed, commenting "I knew you had it in you! Good to know you haven't lost your touch, Darling!"

Her comment warmed the heart of the well-read shopkeeper rather a lot. It excited him a little too, at the end of a long hard day. Lights switched to "Off", they went upstairs. Together. The 39 stairs. Sandra first, then Martin close behind, like really close, the remaining stiff card in his hands.

The following morning, having risen early, he saw that the first of the stickers had been stuck on, by someone. Martin had been so busy at the till that he had not even noticed who had done this but there against the one saying that you should be nicer to your neighbours was a very clear and unmistakable green sticker. Yes, it would be in green of course, Martin took that first colour as a very good sign. A few minutes later a well-dressed Asian man in a beige lightweight suit buying a newspaper had placed a red sticker against the one saying that we should all treat each other with "unconditional positive regard". He commented to Martin,

"Nice chart you have there, Martin my friend. I'll tell all of my friends from the Temple to come in and make their choices, shall I?"

"Now what an excellent idea, yes please do, Mr Singh" came the reply, a broad smile on the face of the innovative English shopkeeper. Sticker three later that morning was from a young boy of just three years of age who had been lifted up by his young mum and who had told her that he liked the yellow sticker colour best and that it needed to go here and so the preferred yellow sticker got stuck firmly on the "Live your life fearlessly in 2019" item. That counts thought Martin, the young man certainly wanted it stuck it on here very deliberately so that was fine by him. Having paid for their Walkers smoky bacon crisps, the yummy mummy herself put her boy down just for a moment of careful reflection and placed an orange sticker against the idea of drivers not driving and using a mobile phone at the same time.

"I think this is a really good idea, mind if I tell my girlfriends from the Cougar gym class to come in and make their choice too? I'm sure they'll buy something from you as well of course!"

This thought warmed Martin too. He did like a good Cougar, especially first thing in the morning. His list was certainly being seen by the Customers then. Mr Singh returned shortly afterwards walking right up to the chart, and without buying anything from the shelves this deliberate man placed a blue sticker very precisely against the idea of changing our political system, smiling again at Martin as he left and nodding his head towards the shopkeeper, in a way suggesting his respect. Words were not spoken between the two men but humans didn't always need words to communicate, right? This was very interesting thought Martin, his day considerably brightened by this very positive experience. Not only were people taking part in this chart with sticker "thing", but one of them had actually just come back into the shop specifically to add a sticker, which surely must mean that he had been thinking about it for some time. How very intriguing. The estate agent and a young attractive brunette lady had also entered the shop together, buying some glossy magazines perhaps for their local branch, and Martin's chart had caught their eye. (I guess "Location, location, location" matters then eh?) They stopped their flirtatious talking and both began to read through the twenty or so ideas up on the poster, while Martin counted their glossy coffee table magazines.

"Now this is really interesting, I do like this" commented Alan. "What's your favourite Helen?" he asked his attractive young companion. Teasingly, she played with the stickers for a few captivating moments, her long-nailed hands rubbing across the shiny surface of the stickers themselves before placing two big reds on one line and a little black triangle very firmly on another below.

"Oh dear, I am being naughty doing that, aren't I, I do hope that's allowed?" she asked Martin, her pretty grey eyes connecting deeply with Martin's soul for a few delightful moments. He gathered himself quickly, the six glossy magazines as well, and replied that this was fine, there were really no rules and he could see no reason why several stickers could not be used on the same item if that mattered to the sticker placer. It hadn't happened yet but she could be the first, yes that was fine, he found himself saying for the fourth time. Interesting that she should have chosen a little triangle too, he thought.

"Well done you" she said, placing her right hand on his cultured arm, "I think it's an awesome idea. We can tell our Prospective Clients to come in if you'd like that?"

Martin would like that very much. And they would.

And so idea of the poster with colourful stickers did its thing, and it gathered real momentum, rather impressive momentum for what was just a large piece of 99p rigid card with bold green writing on it. It had become a bit of a celebrity in its own right. People spoke about it on the high street, and they often said to him that they would recommend it to their friends, colleagues, clients, customers and acquaintances generally. Irony made an appearance too as Martin soon ran out of stickers and did the thing that he just hated doing so much which was to walk round down the road a few shops to the new WH Smith and go in and buy some more stickers there.

Inevitably, as it was WH Smith, the staff were rude and unfriendly and looked away from their customer's deep green eyes, and they didn't even know if they sold stickers there but he found them there himself soon enough and got out as rapidly as he could. They get more like Woolworths in here he thought as he left the cold shadow of their ubiquitous shop, and we all know what happened to Woolies don't we? Imagine not even knowing what stock you have in your own shop! That had never happened in Martins in many years of successful local "know-your-customers well" business. He knew exactly what he had and where it was.

Sandra had placed her stickers too one evening that same week, big orange ones. So too had the local vicar, recently arrived from the parish of Bushey, who said that if it was all right with Martin she would use his chart as inspiration for her next Sunday sermon about the New Year and how we could all learn to break last year's bad habits. He was flattered, though not a religious man in any way. The local lawyer had also come in one lunch time and he had read through the list with great care, (of course what else?) He said that he too liked the idea, that he would weight up the possibilities and would return "in good time" with his measured decision. That would be fine Martin had commented, he had found himself using that phrase rather a lot since the appearance of the chart in his shop. By the way, he had now given his chart the name of "Janus" secretly, named after the two-faced Roman god he had read about in that book. The local butcher had also seen it one morning and definitely disagreed with the idea of eating less animals and he selected to place his large red sticker on the anti-norovirus handwash idea. Sensible man, after all one man' meat is another man' poison.

"Don't talk to me about that bloody virus mate, my Christmas turkey sales were well affected by that bloody thing being passed round. Everyone changed to sausages and chops, I've never known a Christmas like it. Anyway, happy new year to you, let's hope it's a good one full of meat, eh?"

That comment from the butcher reminded Martin that he had agreed to pick Sandra up from work later that evening. Irony made a second appearance when the local Citizen newspaper photographer Paul came round one lunchtime to interview Martin and to take his photograph for their next edition. So he had finally got into local the paper after all then with his New Year resolution idea chart thingy but not in the way that he had first thought of. Martin would be seen on page three by hundreds of local people standing proudly next to "The Janus Chart", proudly inviting the local population "To change their ways in 2019". Paul had said to Martin that it might be best not to go public about the Janus chart name, you know what local school kids can be like. He could foresee comments like "Let's go round to the sweet shop and see that man's anus!" and all that kind of thing, so it was widely agreed that the name was changed. Best to just call it "Martin's Chart".

Martin the man felt proud as he took cash from his customers buying the local paper the following week saying to them:

"I hope you won't mind me mentioning it but I'm on page three, with the chart that you can see here up on the wall next to you?"

They were all very impressed, and more bright colourful stickers were applied, although Martin was now using new ones that he had since ordered in a bulk order from his regular wholesale supplier. Purple, white, pink and light green were now available, and the chart was looking more like a Christmas tree by the day. Yes, his chart with colourful stickers thing was quite something now, with the idea of us never driving a car while using a mobile phone being the high street's number one preferred idea for 2019, in the number one spot by a country mile. Next was the notion of taking time to get to know your neighbours better, closely followed by dog owners clearing up their dogs' mess better, with the ideas or reading more and taking time to meditate more frequently in joint fourth place. Rising up the charts very steadily recently was the anti-norovirus hand wash idea. Was it coincidence he wondered that the dog mess ideas attracted stickers in brown, the mobile phone/driving ideas seemed to attract red stickers only, perhaps "red for danger" he had thought, and that the reading and meditating had only been given stickers in both dark and light green. What did it say he reflected, about how people associated colours with certain activities in life? Perhaps the connection between green and personal growth was exactly right then since reading and meditation looked to be considered as very green activities. Something else he noticed was that once someone had begun with a particular colour sticker on one line, the next person seemed to think that they should stay with that same colour. One of Sandra's colleagues had come in early one morning and had asked if he had any of the blue stickers left as they had run out, so that she could place that same colour against an idea that only had blue stickers next it. People, eh?

'Oh, so you're Martin then, are you? Your Sandra has told me all about you! Lovely idea Babe."

She winked at him as she left his shop, causing him to spill his milky tea all over the Daily Mail.

Martin the newsagent also noticed how some of the bigger intellectual ideas had failed to get any stickers at all, things like living your life fearlessly for instance. This line had not seemed to make a connection with people at all, nor the ideas of listening to classical music each day or of making your life exceptional in 2019. Perhaps people were more focused on local day to day things that they could most easily relate to rather than the more grandiose thoughts.

By January the 6th, Janus was looking a little tired even for a celebrity Roman god. The chart was pretty filled up, very colourful mind, but some of the stickers had begun to peel off slightly with the heat from the radiator nearby and some of them might even soon fall to the floor under the effect of the heat. Imagine that, a great classical deity having its power taken away by a cheap £17.99 white radiator from B&Q! So in line with the twelve days of Christmas idea, Martin and Sandra had both decided in the morning that the chart had nearly had its time and that it would come down after closing the shop for business later that same evening, on the 6th. It had been very interesting and it had been great fun to do too.

It had even got him into the local paper as a result, which encouraged people to buy the local paper from him which had boosted his profits still further over that holiday period. He liked the commercial symmetry of that, did Martin. But the great chart of life had one more surprise still up its little sleeve for Martin. For the local drama group were close to performing the first night of their annual pantomime.

This year the new director was taking the group away from their traditional "Widow Twankie" sort of show, and had written something very individual and very much more modern. It would not be to everyone's taste but others would love it for sure. It had a large cast let's just say. So one Thursday evening shortly before close, many of the actors had walked into his shop fully dressed in costumes from a photo shoot in the local hall further along the high street, getting some exciting pictures for their drama group's website. Another five minutes later and Martin would have shut up shop, but they had just made it in time. He stood there with his cup of tea in his left hand, with full cream milk of course, a little tired towards the end of another long day in retail thinking about shutting up. In utter disbelief he watched as Superman, Harry Potter, Shrek, Hagred, CatWoman, Little Mix and finally Michael McIntyre all walked into his modest shop just to place their stickers personally on his now famous chart. They all did so and promptly left without saying even a word to him, only for the door to open again just ten seconds later as Barack Obama, Lady Gaga, Lord Voldermort, Elvis Presley, two grey aliens, Ghandi and finally God himself came in and did exactly the same thing on the humble shopkeeper's chart. Then they all walked back out, except for God that is, who stayed and slowly turned to the humble shopkeeper and said:

"Hello Mate, Daily Mail and twenty woodbines please, and I'm feeling lucky, so I'll buy a scratch hard too if that's all right with you. I've only got a twenty, that all right?"

Martin took the money from God with earthly courtesy, smiling and said nothing. There were no words.

As God left his humble shop, Martin went over to the door, locked it four times and turned round the Open/Closed sign on the window, and then lowered the shop lights gently. He climbed the stairs, tea mug still in hand and a cheeky Terry's Chocolate Orange in the other, and he called up to the lovely Sandra:

"I say, Sister, stick the kettle on would you please, you'll never believe who just walked into my modest little shop!"

4. Life at the top

"My God, you poor, poor, dear little souls", he said to himself. "It's actually true, you really do look like ants! Brown little ants." And they certainly did from where he was standing. They looked just like ants below. Well they would do wouldn't they when you were looking down on them from an office high up on the 69th floor. Far, far below, the busy little people scurried around the grubby hot streets of New York, running, and rushing and bumping into each other, blinded completely by an absolute belief that what they were all doing actually mattered in some way. It didn't, it oh so didn't, but as long as they were not aware of this tragic fact, then that was just fine for the others high above them, just fine for their lofty superiors up high above.

"At least ants have developed the impressive ability to know how not to bump into each other", he thought, nodding his head in disdainful disbelief at their empty pointlessness, a full sixty nine levels below his silent air-conditioned office. It was one of the many advantages of being so far removed from the grey insignificant masses below that not only did they seem deliciously tiny and remote, but that the sounds from below did not actually travel all the way to his fleshy pig-like ears where he was watching them from. Oh, it was true that the noise of an occasional white or red emergency vehicle below could just about be heard, as the noise of its shrill siren climbed up towards you, but the truth was that even that sounded a whole city away from where he watched from. It was like the radio was on very, very quietly in the background in the next room from him, barely audible, but making a slightly irritating noise that you could not completely block out of your head.

But that was it, other than that, the ants far below him moved around busily but were in effect the silent type. None of their vacuous conversations could be heard up above, nor their tedious fears, goals and ambitions, nor any of their incessant rhythmic breathing as they went about their ignorant business of being. Of being ants.

"Hmm, have you ever seen the movie Antz, oh little people? You know the one where the endearing little ants live in this huge, huge world, with strange threatening creatures invading from time to time, and at the very end of the movie as the camera steadily pulls back out of their world, we see what they really are. Nothing more than tiny ants living amongst the garbage of New York's Central Park! Did they know that was where they lived, in a public park? Fuck no. Did they know anything? Hell no. Ants are the terrestrial version of the pretty but dumb goldfish going round and round in a glass bowl, finding something new at every turn, when there just can't possibly be anything new there at all, ever! It's always the same glass bowl that you're in oh little fishy, the same room, even the same water and pump, the same table and same carpet, durr!! There can be nothing new for you, there just can't be, instead there is only the perfection of the transparent circular trap that you live your short fishy life in, made of manmade glass.

Does that goldfish ever stop to think who provides him with clean water in the bowl once every two weeks? Does he ever question who cleans his filter out every month, who turns the light on in the morning, or who pays for the electricity?

Or whose big hands they are that attend to him, who made the glass bowl that is his fishy little world, or who made the person who made the glass bowl, and who made them?

Or who built the house that the family lives in, who built the wooden table that his bowl stands on, and so on? Nope, that would be asking too much for a pretty but dumb goldfish. Pretty yes, and made available in a great colour, but swimming in utter piscatorial ignorance. He doesn't know what he doesn't know.

"I never really thought how alike ants and goldfish are", the big Executive said to himself, a slight smile appearing at the corner of his smug podgy face. "One is brown and the other is a pretty orange, but both are utterly pointless creatures. Why even bother making them? I mean just why?"

He took a sip of his extremely expensive Columbian coffee from his $1,000 porcelain coffee cup and raised the cup sharply in a patronising gesture to the pointless people below, down to all of the ants. Down there, he thought, the tourists would still be asking for directions to the famous Wall Street, some would want to see the New York Stock Exchange while others would be there just to see the head offices of those huge and faceless financial organisations that eat so many people alive and devour their souls every working day.

Many of them would rush straight to see the famous brass bull of Wall Street, which dear reader is actually not on Wall Street itself, but a block away. This was the bull that had come to symbolize corporate greed and excess over the years, or rather as he liked to call it personally, "Success". He liked that "excess" sounded similar to "success". Most of the tourists flocking to New York like to have their photo taken standing by the iconic bull, some from the front, and others from the rear where its impressive highly polished brass "cojones" can just be held in both hands, as you smile into the latest and talented iPhone camera. So many Japanese hands had held and then rubbed the bull's balls for photographic purposes that they shone bright on an East Coast morning from as far as one hundred yards away.

And that was not bullshit.

Mr Executive finished his very fine coffee, put his summer weight jacket on and walked over to the elevator. There he would shortly be taken up to the helipad a further five levels up, whisked there vertically in fifteen seconds precisely in air-conditioned executive silence, to be greeted very personally by "Miss Behaving" as he had come to refer to his preferred brunette personal assistant. She would immediately be allowed to go through their regular procedure. She was to take his attaché case from his right hand into her left, and to lead him to the copter two paces ahead and to his right at all times. She was to open the door for Mr Successful to climb into his sumptuous tan leather seat, before receiving permission via a verbal grunt to return his case to him with both hands and to place it firmly on his lap. No eye contact whatsoever was to be made with him, not under any circumstances, even for a brief moment. To do so, was written into her contract as gross misconduct and constituted an offence for which she would surely be dismissed, and immediately. Not what you might want to have happen to you when you are seventy four floors up, and in the presence of a cold, egotistical, financially motivated and uncaring man. For seventy four floors up, anything could happen.

"Is there anything else I can do for you, (she was to pause now for three seconds exactly) Mr Jones?" she was then always to ask.

As was always the tradition, there was no comment returned to her, not even a grunt, he only looked ahead, and her final words to him that morning, for which he paid her handsomely, were to be:

"Have a very successful trip, (a three second pause again was stipulated) Sir".

With that, she was allowed to close his door firmly, ensuring three times as per his manual command that the door of the magnificent multi-million dollar flying machine was fully, safely and properly closed. His hands were never to touch anything as germ-laden as a common all-helicopter door handle. He picked up some white surgical gloves, size medium, that were made available to him in a side pocket and put them on particularly slowly. Next he took a small plastic bag from the chilled refrigerator box and carefully took out a set of brand new Bose headphones and microphone set from the same bag, placing them slowly onto his own head so as to be in contact with his preferred pilot, aka "Casey Jones the engine driver". Miss Behaving was to stand respectfully on the white line by the elevator shaft with her hands behind her back out of complete and unquestioning respect for her all-knowing employer as she waited. It even used those words in the contract. Even if her long hair was to wave in the breeze, or her stipulated short black skirt was to ride up in the breeze too revealing her required underwear, hands were to assume the required position. She was paid extra for that little piece of discipline, for it mattered to him you see.

Greatly. It mattered greatly to him you see.

He would turn his head round in her direction very deliberately at that point. And stare coldly.

At his command, a "Proceed" instruction was spoken only to his trusted pilot, and only then, could his ocean blue and aluminium helicopter be given permission by him to leave the helipad, flying even higher over all of the grubby brown ants far, far below.

For Mr Jones had big business to attend to that day. He had people to see. Deals to close. And ants were just not his thing.

Nor pretty orange goldfish.

5. Human Obsolesence

Peter used to drive an Audi. Peter liked his Audi very much. For the record it was an Audi A6 saloon, and it was a two point four litre petrol model with the automatic gearbox, if you like to know that level of engine and transmission detail.

It was in a lovely silver colour, with a rich deep blue leather interior and he drove it for a little over eight years. The leather was a very high quality "Nappa" leather by the way. It was a very comfortable car, with nice things like heated seats, in both the front and the rear. It offered lovely leather headrests and leather front and rear arm rests too, and being an Audi it came with a very classy interior. It had fine things fitted as standard like air-conditioning.

So Peter kept his quality Audi for a little over eight years, until it had covered a shade over 112,000 miles. That was nothing for a big Audi built in Germany. Great car. They made them really well over there. These cars are built to last. Almost like a tank, one might say.

What he enjoyed most about his German executive saloon was what they refer to as "build quality". This is not just about how well the car was put together in the original factory in the first place, nor is it even just about the quality of the individual components like interior switches, knobs and door handles.

You see, it's really more about the thinking and the design that was behind the car when it was first drawn up. It's particularly about the level of commitment to quality that the team of engineers and designers decided to invest in the car before they had even made their first mock-up models in clay. It's about their end goal. In the case of the Audi, that commitment had been very good right across the team and from the very beginning of the project. Consistent with their thorough Audi reputation, they had decided that the car would be a high quality product at the end of the design process. And there should be no compromise.

What this meant for all of the Peters of the World buying their lovely Audi A6 was that the commitment to quality would filter down from the design and build process fully into the ownership stage of the car's life, and that is exactly what happened. What you don't know is that Peter was the third owner of the car, buying it when it had driven something like twenty eight thousand miles, and it felt solid from the first day that he drove it until its last day in his possession. He found this to be a great car. Well, she was made in Germany after all where they produce many excellent motor cars.

Their marketing people like to refer to cars like these as "Life Partners" since they could stay with an individual owner or a family for example for ten, twenty or even thirty years, such was their fine build quality. Other manufacturers whose cars also fitted into this category include BMW, Mercedes, Saab, Volvo, all joining Audi of course. Sadly for the British car industry brands such as Jaguar didn't really quite fit in to this elite group quite yet, shame, but soon perhaps. Land Rover were making sound progress in this area too.

Now, over time any car will begin to show its age. That's not to say that it will stop working, or that it will begin to fail to do the job of transportation that it has always done so well, but that it will start to appeal to an owner or a potential buyer a little less than it once did.

The car-buying customer has become what we may call "savvy". Even very good design will be familiar to the eye of the buying public after a while and they will want their cars to evolve, to improve and to change a little so that they are visually fresh. All car manufacturers are painfully aware of this, so too are companies that manufacture vans and trucks and trains, airplanes and computers too of course for that matter. Perhaps even motorcycles as well, and certainly modern smartphones. Time is sadly the enemy even of the very finest design. There are actually two cars that have succeeded in defying this golden rule, and those are the Citroen DS and the Jaguar E-Type that still look as good today as they did on the day of their official launch over fifty years ago. But there again as we all know these two cars were both designed personally by God, so that doesn't count! "La Deese" even means "Goddess" in French so there's your proof!

For the rest of the mortal-designs, they have to be acceptably good visually in the first place and then kept fresh and what is called "current". European manufacturers will generally bring out a model that will last about five maybe six years, before the next version or replacement model comes out around then. They might tweak and change external things like the car's light clusters, or the style of its wheel trims or some detail on the inside of the car, things like that, but the public will generally be very used to seeing that car around on the roads for about five maybe six years. Now, it must be said that not everyone quite takes this same approach. The Japanese car manufacturers for example also keep their models fresh and "current" with similar facelifts, but their models are designed to be out for a much smaller period of time of just three years, before they launch the next version then. This means that as they are launching a brand new model, so another team perhaps in the very same offices are also starting work on its successor already. No car manufacturer can afford to get the next model badly wrong, and so for this reason this is a very pressurised three year process where they have to bring out a car that is widely agreed to be superior to its predecessor, that keeps ahead somehow of the competition's range of models, and which stays within the latest environmental regulation, and fully so. As if that was not a big enough challenge they have to make sure that they keep as many of their existing customers too as they are more easy to sell a new model to than people who drive another brand. Once we have made a choice of car brand that we are happy with, it has been found through research that it is somewhere between two and eight times harder to get us to switch over to another brand. So you really, really want to keep as many of your existing customers as you can, for sure! It's a pretty tough challenge overall, at least the greater cycle of six years gives you much more time within which to get your next product right than the shorter three year Japanese product cycle.

Now, back to Peter, actually let's call him Pete shall we as we're getting to know him a little better now. What Pete had come to realise with his gorgeous Audi was that even that high quality car of his needed to be serviced and maintained over time of course, just like a Ford or a Toyota or a Honda. Even though it was well built, even a fine German Audi has bits that will wear down over time, albeit more slowly than another company's product. It too will need to be replaced at some point. Being a bit of an enthusiast, Pete knew that car manufacturers could make their cars of an even higher quality if they had to, but then again the car's price would be much greater. There was a commercial balance to be found, as you may know.

Rolls Royce, Bentley and perhaps Aston Martin are considered to make truly fine driving machines in a higher category of quality. General wear and tear over time wears down even the best vehicle, gearboxes need replacing, electric systems start to fail and something awful delivered by the Devil himself called "rust" can start to eat the car alive. It used to be called "TinWorm". How well the Italian car industry knows this last point! The miles driven and the time on the road will both slowly take from the car, any car, and the manufacturers know this of course. They want you to enjoy their car, but they don't want this to go on for ever otherwise you will never come back and buy another one from them! Their cars are built to last a certain time, or perhaps a certain mileage before you throw it away and buy its replacement.

So, welcome to a thing that's called Obsolescence. The company behind your mobile phone will be equally familiar with this concept too. Ask Apple or Samsung. Obsolescence, remember that word, it matters hugely these days.

Pete was now in his fifties and he felt that the same ageing process that happens to our cars also happens to the people that make them. Or drive them. He was lucky in that he enjoyed very good health, although like all of us he could never tell what lay ahead round the corner on the great M25 motorway of life of course. But even now, he could sense where he was in his own life, and what the likely percentage of his life now experienced was statistically likely to be versus what lay ahead.

He was therefore in no doubt that he was well into the second half of his life, and that he was probably about sixty to sixty five percent of the way through his current life on this planet. He still had huge amounts of energy left in him, and he was sure that intellectually speaking his best years still lay ahead of him. He had noticed Obama use that phrase to great effect in his campaigns and he found it rather inspiring. He had many books to write yet, possibly a play or two in him too, and at a very great stretch maybe just one situation comedy programme as well. For they are really hard to get right. He considered that he had a good sense of humour, and one that was certainly above the average "GSOH" and he enjoyed greatly watching and listening to the world and its people going on around him.

Young Pete had been blessed with strong powers of observation, (possibly exceptional ones although he didn't go public with that idea ever because it sounded too boastful.) He was a regular runner, and he had been since he was still in the sixth form at school. It was an important part of Pete's life balance "thing" not to smoke or to drink alcohol and to go running on alternative days. Sometimes he ramped that back up to six days a week, his right knee condition allowing. That way he would average about fifteen runs a month minimum, which was about one hundred and eighty runs a year, give or take a few evenings when he may not been able to go out for various reasons. He felt, (and make a note here dear reader if you will please that Pete "felt" things a lot), that this level of physical activity probably made a significant contribution to his personal physical health. It felt logical to him that it did, anyway.

It also definitely contributed to his psychological wellbeing, he was pretty sure of that too. The overall combination of not smoking tobacco and not drinking alcohol and being a committed runner appealed to him overall as a lifestyle. However, like his Audi wearing down over time, he too was slowing. His natural running speed had dropped by a colossal twenty per cent now that he was in his fifties when compared to his natural running speed in his early forties. Twenty whole percent! Even worse for young Pete, was the certain knowledge that his pace would only erode still further. It was only going to go one way. It was a source of some real concern for him, and one that gave rise to not a little depression from time to time, usually in the Winter. For going for a run had become a part of this healthy man.

But, at the same time he knew that he could do little if anything about it. Some things are within our control and others not, right? He had also recently experienced some dizzy spells, and a couple of them had been quite unpleasant. A visit to his reasonably helpful local doctor had suggested that Pete probably had some kind of vertigo, or at least an inner ear infection. That kind of thing would have been unthinkable ten years ago but it was now a reality for this man.

Even worse than that, was that back in the April of that year he had experienced groin pain over several weeks and had been diagnosed with a hernia! A small routine operation had taken place that same month which had gone well and he had made a good recovery in under a week, but this was Pete! Pete had never once had weaknesses like hernias or dizzy spells or a slowdown in his jogging speed! He wasn't a smoker. He rarely drank alcohol. He followed a strong pescatarian diet. Pete didn't do illness and weaknesses! He was a good man, and a healthy one at that. He didn't like how it made him feel. Like his solid six cylinder Audi, he was a great example of the model.

But he did now, and it frustrated him greatly. Remember that word obsolescence? This was the same process of obsolescence that had started to affect his immortal silver Audi, beginning to do the same to him, and Pete didn't like this one bit.

He could fight with it a little, in order to push back on it, but he knew that the flow of the tide was not in his favour, not these days. Time would always come out on top. It happens to us all, just like it does to an Audi, even to Pete's glorious silver Audi.

6. Job Description for a Human Being

- Our ref. 600900736/2013

1ST February 2023

Dear New Human Being,

I am delighted to offer you the position of baby junior human being. This offer is with immediate effect.

Your general place of work will be the Planet Earth where you will be required to be on duty, fully alive and breathing for twenty four hours a day, and for three hundred and sixty five days of your human calendar year. The breathing will happen very naturally, it is not something that you will need to think about in a conscious manner, thus allowing you to concentrate on other significant matters. You may select what those matters are to be. We will have no influence on your choices. The precise location of work will be entirely yours. It may change throughout your life.

At this point in what you will come to call "Time" we regret to inform you that we are not in a position to be able to confirm to you the precise number of years over which the position will continue to be made available to you. One never knows. We do, but it is not yours to know. Nor, regrettably, are we able to offer you any kind of estimate or guess of the same in advance. Don't you and your rather simple two-part head-located pink gum-like brain go worrying about this last point, there really is no need. Nor is there any point. Millions of earth years of experience of offering similar positions to other human babies before your arrival in your world have led us to believe that it's just best that you don't know this information. It remains our very firm belief that prior knowledge of the length of your terrestrial existence would in fact almost certainly spoil your time on your planet. "Ours to know, yours not to know" is a helpful approach we have found. We're sure that you will understand.

Please observe this rule carefully at all times. There is no Right of Appeal on your part.

You will be provided with one head-based computer called a brain, a level of awareness that will evolve rapidly over time and a strong sense of considerable opportunity laying ahead of you. We are not able to guarantee the maximisation of any such opportunity that may arise in your life on the planet by the way. We are sure that you will understand this too.

All of the above will be provided to you free of charge, and you will not be required at any time to reimburse your creator for any of the above tools. Quite a deal, don't you think? They are made available for you to use to best effect, as you deem appropriate. We will also provide you with some basic skills and attributes for you to build on as you deem appropriate throughout your time here on Planet Earth.

If it helps we recommend that you lead your life based on the "three score and ten years" time model, - that is about seventy years in total.

It can be more, but then again it could be less. A lot less sometimes. In no way does this number model constitute a commitment to you for this length of time.

If there is any change to this number you may possibly be informed of this change through your physical body and the personal changes noted by you (or others) therein. However, the Cosmology Company can make no undertaking that this will always be so. Keep an eye out for them though if you are able to, (you have been given two eyes after all), the signs may be missed all too easily in some cases. Tragically so sometimes. And Good Earth "Luck" with it all.

We take this opportunity to congratulate you on getting this position in the first place. Statistically, the chances of this ever happening to you at all were very greatly stacked against you. You are a minor miracle. Sadly, it is a harsh fact of life for human beings on the planet Earth that too many of you don't even have the position held open to them for even a few days, let alone seventy or more human years. We would refer you to the troubled continent that you call Africa by way of very clear evidence of this last fact.

The role that we are giving you is a completely individual one. You are unique, and truly so. You will be influenced by the two humans that brought you into the world it is true, and you will carry many of their characteristics. This will apply to physical attributes for example such as the colour of your hair growing on your head, to your height and even the quality of your eyesight. Much of what may be called your "Personality" has already long, long been determined from before your birth from out of the human womb. However, the single greatest challenge for you now must surely be to make some sense of the world that you are born into and of your place within it. Rise to that challenge as best you might, My Young Human Being.

Incidentally, the two people that you will come to know as your "parents" may or may not be there to raise you as you grow older. They too come and go I can confirm. In some cases of adoption, they may not even be your actual birth parents. Even if they are present as you grow and develop, there may possibly be no blood relationship between you, although there is such a connection in most cases. The length in human time of the offer of life made to your "Parents" may not be guaranteed either.

Our terms are that "Personal circumstances will vary, and life patterns may be recorded for training purposes, terms and conditions apply, your life may be at risk if you do not keep up a healthy commitment to your body, home and life."

Be brave, be strong and whatever your chosen path look forward whenever you can, and not backwards, for you will see no good road to travel on behind you. There is a good reason why you are supplied with a human face on the front of your head that faces forward. Under no circumstances will you be permitted to travel back in "Time". Such an act will be deemed to be a violation of Nature and of the Cosmic Rules.

Existence amongst other humans may mean that things around you will change. That Change may be great on occasions. Get used to the continuous presence of Change as soon as you can. Little will stay the same in your Life on this planet. Your planet is in a state of relentless flux. You must quickly adapt and be able to respond to this thing you will call Change. It will always be around you, though not always obviously so.

Sometimes you will in fact be aware of it, other times oblivious to it, whilst on other occasions you may yourself be the Bringer of Change to those around you. You have much ahead of you.

At other times it may suit the purpose of those same others around you that some changes should be kept from your eyes very deliberately and for as long as possible. Beware the motives and drives of your fellow humans. All is not as it may seem, Young Human.

Change may be evidenced throughout your life in many ways. For example in your physical body, in the views that you hold on human intellectual arguments and indeed on the very things that you find yourself looking for in your lonely earth-bound and individual existence. Be comfortable with change young human, embrace it well and learn to go with the river's flow. For it flows out to the sea and not without good reason.

Be independent in your thinking as freely as you wish to be. You would do well to acquire early the wisdom to know which battles you should fight, and which not. Not all may be won by you, nor will they be. Please note that Healthcare Insurance is not to be made available to you under this offer, and the Great Creator above can take no responsibility whatsoever for any illnesses, be they awkward, embarrassing, painful, restrictive, terminal or otherwise that may befall you. This includes both physical and psychological complaints, and in the second half of your life only, spiritual ones as well.

There is no official grievance procedure. Monetary expenses many not be claimed for from the Great Creator under any circumstances, whatsoever. All such life expense claims must be handled on a local planetary level only. To that end, network well within your community and develop good relationships with your fellow humans. This investment is likely to pay off in the longer-term, should you be around for the longer-term that is, which as per the paragraph above may not be guaranteed by the Cosmology Company in any way whatsoever.

Trade union membership will be allowed across all members of the planet wishing to partake, as will the membership of all professional bodies, training associations and social groups. This will include what you will come to know as Facebook, LinkedIn and Twitter. However, at the end of your finite time on the planet, such memberships will not count particularly in your favour. They will all be relinquished too upon completion of your mission on the planet. The same applies to any religious, agnostic or atheist groups that you choose to join. However, a sustained period of membership of green, environmental or Wildlife groups may be looked on very favourably at the final reckoning. Heed this last point well.

For a reckoning there will be. No confirmation can be given on the date of this last event, but come it will, and sometimes when it is least expected. You would do well to make note of this certainty, but you won't of course, not if you're like the rest of your race.

The older you get you will be surprised to learn that the less you know. This will be a source of great pain for you in your later life. Perhaps a more accurate way of saying this is that the older you grow so you will become aware of quite how much there is in the world around you to try to understand. Others will try to impose their ideas and entire "Systems of Belief" onto you in an attempt to control and stifle the wonderful person that you may become. You will be faced with a choice of how to respond.

Remember that human time is not on your side and opportunities will be closed in your face just as a window of timber may close in the simple house in which you live. Choose wisely, for there will always be consequences. Both for you and for others around you.

At times you will be troubled. You will need what is called "Help" or "Assistance". You may find the need to gain advice from your fellow man/woman. Sometimes you will know who to turn to, on other occasions you will feel a drive to make your own choices, whatever the consequences of such a decision. All men and women make their mark on this world, as does a simple pen filled with black ink writing on a clean sheet of white paper. For that is the very nature of human existence, to endeavour, to try, and to make what you may come to call "An Effort".

Nothing more. Simply that.

There is no alternative, you are required to join in the game, and to do so at the time not of your choosing but of ours only. The company also reserves the right to decide the location and circumstances of your existence and any changes therein. We are sure that you will understand. You will have no Right of Appeal.

The "Deck of playing cards" that is given to you, you are to play that hand as best you can. Under the general terms and conditions of life on the planet, the cards may not be swapped, exchanged, traded or refunded in any way. The management's decision is final and may not be challenged at all in any way, including verbally, in writing or on an Apple iPad, on any other Tablet Computer including the Amazon Fire & the Google Pixel, on a Kindle or on a now-classic Blackberry or on the Microsoft Surface tablet device (version 1.0 onwards).

You will also be provided with a Basic Personal Conscience ("BPC") with which to go about your life. This is a remarkably powerful tool made available to each and every one of you. Use it wisely, young Human. Again this will be provided to you free of charge and you will not be required to return this to your Creator. At the time of your physical end, it may be taken away from you soon after Physical Death of the Body ("PDB") and taken to a safe place of storage, along with billions of other consciences in the infinitely large Cerebral Warehouse of Life ("CWL").

Please note that travel expenses to and from this sacred place may not be claimed under any circumstances, nor will location maps of this amazing warehouse ever be made available publically, nor to you personally. To reveal its possible location to others, would constitute a breach of contract and deemed to be gross misconduct. Termination may follow at a time of our choice. We are sure that you will understand. You may have no Right of Appeal.

In summary, Young Human, congratulations on coming into what you will refer to rather simplistically as "Existence".

We welcome you to this world, and we look forward to watching your progress with great interest, individually monitoring you regularly on an hourly basis - but you will very quickly forget this last fact as it's just best that way. As you will like to term it, a lot of your mind will have been "Wiped".

And please note that we have rather a lot of experience at this old game ..... older than your model can even comprehend, we'll leave it at that.

Work hard junior human, learn well and observe much around you for local knowledge is a highly valuable commodity on your extraordinary planet.

Above all, and finally, respect the One who goes by the name of "Sir David Attenborough", at all times. Love that Man.

With our warmest wishes, be back in touch with you again ... well, sometime soon,

G

Mr G

<u>Senior Demi-God of On-surface Human Resources</u> (permanent appointment)

7. The X1Vth Annual International Security Conference

"Yes Ma'am, how may I help you?"

"I'll take a coffee thank you, but it's not to be too strong okay. You have low-fat cream right?"

"Sure, I'll get that for you right away ma'am".

The efficient young American waiter immediately got on with the single given task of providing his important customer with an excellent cup of morning coffee, not too strong, and with low-fat milk as we call it here in the UK. Months of training, and being coached individually by his up-market hotel chain employer had taught him the importance of instantly committing to memory the chosen drink that had just been ordered by his Customer. To replay it out loud to his customer and ask for her confirmation only risked irritating her. That would be simply unacceptable in this glamorous hotel with its high international profile to maintain. After all, this was not a branch of the ubiquitous Starbucks chain.

He took a fine white porcelain cup and matching saucer in his gloved hands, also in pristine white, and poured the Colombian coffee carefully into the vessel, added the warm low-fat milk, and noticing that the lady was holding her special security edition Blackberry in her right hand, passed the cup professionally towards her available left hand, and at exactly the correct speed. Good detail, for this was where Training paid off. Coffee was never to be thrust into place but instead it was to be gently placed, at all times. Spillage onto the saucer was also unacceptable and would surely be noted by the watching head waiter. She seemed to appreciate this very much, she moved the smart phone to the inside pocket of her tweedy jacket, smiling ever so slightly at the muscular handsome young man. She had been quietly studying how well ironed his shirt was across his toned chest, and although the coffee table prevented her seeing the lower half of his athletic body, she felt sure that his shoes would have been highly polished, and only in official black of course.

"Wonderful, thank you so much young man" she replied.

"Have a nice day ma'am, and be sure to come and see us here at The International again"

the young professional replied, holding her gaze just a little, before turning to meet the needs of his next Customer with immaculate grace and sheer professionalism. A robot could not have performed better. He had done well, and she was nicely satisfied by him.

The well-dressed lady walked towards the main conference hall, coffee cup in hand, and was stopped for the fourth time in just a few minutes for a final security check before being allowed to enter the huge golden auditorium. The black male security guard politely offered to take her coffee for her, as a young black female colleague stepped forward to body search their important visitor and to politely look through her black leather Mulberry handbag, with her permission naturally first requested. Again this was where Training paid off.

She also took her Blackberry from her, taking off the back casing and removing the battery to check for anything that may have been hidden inside, before neatly putting it all back together with gloved hands on the desk in front of her and handing it back to its rightful owner. White gloves again, just like the athletic young waiter.

"Thankyou ma'am, you're good to go."

"Have a nice day with us ma'am" replied the male security guard, passing the coffee cup back to the lady delegate, quite well but not quite as well as the young waiter a few yards away would definitely have done. There was a little more thrust here than polite placing, but he got it good enough.

Mrs Azani proceeded into the main hall and was personally greeted by yet another security professional who asked to see her badge. She was specifically interested in the "DSN" as it was known in the security industry. She scanned the number of F17 into a little reader held in her right hand, pressed the earpiece in her right ear, and spoke softly into a discrete microphone concealed in her jacket lapel.

"DSN F17 to her seat now, DSN F17. Please follow me ma'am" she said as she took Mrs Azani personally to her seat.

"Rest rooms are along the corridor to your right ma'am, you will need to be accompanied by one of my colleagues should you choose to leave whilst The President is speaking to the room".

"Yes of course, I understand" the lady in seat F17 replied, as she took her seat, smiling and introducing herself to old international security and political friends already sat either side of her. It was good to be here and to see them again. It had been a few years.

More important people were being shown to their seats now too, some with coffee cups in their hands, some with their cups being held for them if they had both hands full already. One very well-dressed man was having his badge re-applied to his jacket lapel as he was seen to be struggling with it a little, the very helpful black female security guard saying:

"Oh here, let me get that for you Sir, they can be a little awkward at times. I guess they don't make them as well as they used to, right?"

He was then very efficiently taken to his correct seat within just a few seconds and recorded as in place with the conference security office above over the lapel microphone system.

"Boy, they sure don't let you hang around too long round here now do they?" he said laughing and turning to the dark-haired guy sitting next to him, easing himself into the huge comfortable blue velour seat.

"I guess not, must be something to do with today's opening speaker maybe?" came the friendly, confident but firm reply.

Most people were in their correct Delegate Security Number seats, DSN you understand, just a few minutes later. The hi-tech all-black earpieces were being put to sound use by the army of security men and women throughout the hall, and final gulps of now warm only coffee were being taken.

Fine porcelain cups and saucers were being placed under chairs in preparation. Throats were cleared, skirts were brushed into place and ties straightened. Packs were opened and agendas were perused, and the few final handshakes and friendly nods of the head from one delegate to another took place amongst the hundreds of participants, before the Caucasian Ambassador purposefully took to the stage. As he walked over to the microphone and stand, in his smartly pressed navy blue suit, immaculate white shirt and medium blue tie, the audience politely applauded him, some smiling too. He was nearing the end of his six month tenure as Chairman and he was generally considered to have done a good job. One or two of the middle eastern delegates thought that their own man would have done a better job, some of the South American delegates thought that his lack of language skills made him a very awkward choice indeed as their international Chairman, but generally he had worked hard and been diplomatic enough to all concerned. For a white, well-educated Eastern seaboard man that is.

At first the microphone did not work, and to the very less important people positioned right at the back of the hall he looked rather odd just standing there probably saying some mighty fine things but with none of his wise words being heard at all, not by them at least. There were gestures made from one delegate to another pointing to the ear, enquiring if anyone around them could hear him. No-one could and there were many nods of the head and shrugs of seriously well-paid shoulders confirming that it wasn't just them who couldn't hear a word that the Ambassador was saying. The Managing Director of the hotel chain sitting somewhere at the back of the hall was both frustrated with the technical hitch, but also quietly delighted at the huge marketing opportunity that was being given to him by today's event. With this important man standing on his hotels' stage apparently saying something vital, and with the plaque saying "The International Welcomes You" and its hotel logo staring back out at the delegates and importantly to the press photographers very clearly, this was an important conference. But he needed the Microphone system to kick in immediately.

No-one dared to interrupt the Chairman, and to tell him the bad news about the microphones or the speakers not working correctly. He seemed to be in full flow anyway, and the sooner that they had let him wobble on, the sooner he would be off the stage giving way to The President, who was going to be the real star of the morning. Just then, the technology did indeed cut in with immaculate timing as the speaker announced:

"... and so it gives me very great pleasure to welcome to the fourteenth Annual International Security Conference, The President of the United States".

Everyone broke in to very loud applause, and the warmth in the chilly hall seemed warm enough and pretty genuine too. As the Chairman returned to the black velour seat that he got as a speaker versus the blue velour of the delegates, the curtain to the side of the stage was opened with great care and in walked The President.

Many people cheered loudly, and shouted "Yes!" and "Whoo!" and "This year he really did come!", and "Now you're talking!" and "Here's the Man himself" and other such supportive comments could be heard all round the stage. There were a few inevitable "Awesome!" comments heard too. The hall rose to its feet, and those fine coffee cups and agendas fell to the floor in a moment of rather unusual excitement and not a little passion too. For this was a very senior and professional audience.

They would generally conduct themselves in exactly the way that you would expect from the elite in the global business of International Security, being reserved, cautious and generally calm. But not today, for the applause continued for a further minute as Barack Obama stood at the speaker's desk, smiling and waving at his select audience before looking down as his notes.

The audience took this as his cue that he wanted to start and so important security bottoms returned to DSN seats and the hall was once again quiet. The President took a sip of water, and he cleared his executive throat.

"Thank you for paying me the honour of inviting me to the X1Vth Annual International Security Conference here in Boston. I come here to pay tribute today to the vitally important work that you and all of the men and women in your organisations do around the world each and every day. You make the world in which we live a safer and better place, and for that I stand here today to thank you, each and every one of you."

The hall smiled uniformly. The delegates approved of how the President had begun. Collective Smugness rose a little, and the temperature of the hall itself seemed to go up a few degrees in just a single moment. Delegates turned to each other and smiled, all feeling very good about each other's superb colleague in the fruitful and wonderfully lucrative world of International Security. It was good to know that their work mattered. Thankyou.

The President continued with his very carefully prepared speech.

"Many of you attending here today have dedicated your lives to the business of security, and have attached your own careers very openly to the business of making the world a more secure place for all of those family, friends and neighbours around you. You are quite simply the best that there is in the business".

The hall was getting positively warm now.

"You have shown that great things can be achieved both domestically and on the global stage when we unite behind a single cause and pull together as you have done. You have shown the world that we can indeed make the world a better place through your dedication".

Smiles, there more smiles, and not a few handshakes amongst the professional delegates.

Standing quietly at the back of the stage was The President's chosen speech writer.

"That was what you call the setup, now here comes the punch" he quietly muttered to himself, his arms folded and one hand lightly covering his face so that no-one could lip read his words.

"And yet", continued the Big Man "I wonder if we get it right all of the time. Many the night when my head hits the pillow in The White House with thoughts of innocent victims going round in my head, victims of overseas war campaigns in countries that most Americans will surely never visit."

The hall's temperature just dropped a full degree lower. Eyebrows raised more than a little, and all round too, just where was he going with this now then?

"Do we do well to march into other territories and do as we think right?

Really?

Do we have any more right to do this than any other country has to march into The United States of America and do it to us? Does the size of our great nation, economically and militarily, not bring us an even greater responsibility to act with the highest level of integrity possible?"

Always an interesting topic that, the one of integrity. The hall froze, precisely where was he going with this?

"Many of you will have studied something that we refer to as Cause and Effect. I know that many of you here today have lectured throughout this great land of ours on this very topic yourselves and have written fine books on it as well. Standing before you here today, I have to tell you that I have a great fear that we may indeed be the very cause of many of the situations that we face around the world today. Yes, we ourselves, we are likely the Cause."

"I realise that this may be very difficult for this conference of distinguished delegates to accept, but my Friends, accept it you must".

And The President, The Big Guy, the Man himself, the whole enchilada, the Big Cheese, the man who actually came to the conference finally in this year, then went on to give all of those comfy, smug, highly paid delegates of the X1Vth Annual International Security Conference both barrels, and head-on too.

They didn't like it of course, not one bit, for their world had just changed, and not one of them had seen it coming. Like the very Missiles of Death that they approved, procured and whose use they sanctioned personally, it flew in out of nowhere. A verbal Exocet, or whatever the latest equivalent may be.

The speech writer at the back smiled, and he raised his eyebrows a little. His job was done for the day. But they had more work to do if they were really going to be the change that the people wanted. More speeches were underway. For this was a very determined President who was intent on making his mark in a way that no other President had done before. He was going to move the goalposts. And widely so. He was going to change the rules. And he was going to bring the Power of America back into the hands of the American people and take it away from the Military Industrial Complex. For it had rested with them for far too long, since President Eisenhower's famous speech on the 17th of January 1961, and he would do whatever it took to return the United States to the People of the United States. The People that he was elected to serve, the People that he was really supposed to be there for. The ones that had put him into power to support them, his Customers if you like.

His next speech at the weekend, would be in New Mexico, where he would talk about Area 51, and about what really happened at Roswell way back in 1947. Significantly important work lay ahead for this ambitious President. And the world knows what things can happen to a young ambitious President if the men in the shadows do not like the nature of that ambition.

8. By the Christmas Tree

Jules had no idea how long he had been standing there.

Nor did he have any real idea what time of the day it was.

Nor actually which day of the week it was.

It was somewhere between six pm and seven pm, and he remembered coming back in from walking their dog an hour or two ago. Just as it was getting dark and he could remember the temperature was beginning to drop.

He was standing on his own in the corner of the family living room. In the low light. By the tree, he was standing by the Christmas tree. Standing on his own.

His mind was elsewhere though, travelling back in time, back to the time when his beautiful and handsome son Nicolas was still very much alive.

In the background he could hear the sound of the rest of the family going about their business in the family kitchen. They made noises with plates and bowls and cutlery. There was a little music on in the background too, Christmas Carols he thought he could recognise. He could just make out the low drone of someone speaking on the telephone somewhere. The mixture of noise was considerable but it was all very normal household noise.

He stood silent. On his own. In the fading Winter light.

He was recalling an event that was anything but normal, the moment when he had been told that their son Nicolas had been caught in an avalanche whilst on a skiing holiday in the French Alps with a group of friends.

They were all beautiful people.

They were all in their early to mid twenties, and had so much to live for. Surely they all had much opportunity ahead of them. And yet a pile of lousy rocks and rubble and dirty snow had caught them up in a few terrifying moments, damaged them badly, spat three of them out alive but kept one of them inside, his cold body only to be found several days later.

Jules stared at the Christmas tree. It was so colourful, and bright and engaging but he only saw through it to the blackness on the other side.

This time last year, he and Nico had been standing here in this very same corner of their living room sharing a bottle of Belgian beer and chatting about the year ahead. He could see clearly the dark green checked button-down collar shirt that his handsome tall young son had definitely been wearing that Christmas Eve. He remembered it well, and the slightly faded blue Levi jeans that his son had also been wearing that evening.

He reached down with his left hand and touched that same green shirt which he was now wearing.

The jeans were still in the house. Nico's mother had washed them. She had ironed them lightly and placed them at the foot of his bed. In the hope that he might somehow arise from the dirty snow that had taken their son's young life and walk back across the green lawn and into their lives again, one warm Spring evening.

He never would of course.

The lightly ironed jeans would not be worn again.

Jules, the lost parent, just stood there, staring through the colours of the tree and into the darkness in the corner of the room.

Sometimes he would nod his head just very slightly, nodding it in pained disbelief.

Just about twelve months ago, their son had been with them all, with his parents, with his sister and their loving dog, in this very same house where they had always lived together. A family, we call it a family.

In this same room.

Same corner in fact.

Same heavy brass pot that this year's Christmas tree stood in too.

Where was the memory of Nicolas their beloved son then? How did that all work, he thought to himself ….

Was it attached to a place, like their house and the corner of the familiar sitting room just here by the Christmas tree? Or was it in fact attached to something else very different, to a point in time?

The sitting room corner was still here like it was last year, but Nico was nowhere to be seen. He had been taken from them.

Brutally fast.

And so his grieving father concluded that people are in their time, that is to say they are connected to a particular spin of the planet and then they are gone. Go back to the geographical location where they once walked, where you think they are and you will see them walk no more.

They've gone.

Snatched, like a fruit from a branch.

That was in a different time that they walked.

That must be the nature of human existence, thought the grieving good man. That we live at a point in time that is determined by other people and other things going on around us, and that period of time is completely unique and it may never be revisited again. Go back to the restaurant where you first met someone special, or to a great hall where you heard an orchestra play and all is quiet once more. The people have moved on, or they have been moved on. The connection between People and Place has been severed.

Yes, his son did once stand here in this same green checked shirt.

But that was then and this was now a different time, a totally different spin of the planet.

And there can be no going back in what we call "Time".

Just then he could sense a slight change in the air, and the door opened respectfully. His wife came in, and she knew just where he would be standing.

Like he was the evening before.

And the evening before that. And so many evenings before too.

For a few moments, they said nothing. They did not turn to look at each other. They rarely did these days. Each knew the other was there though.

She spoke first, and she spoke softly.

"It hurts all the time doesn't it?"

"Yes" he replied in a whisper.

"Are you coming through to eat something?" her voice a little stronger than his.

"You go, I may come through later. I just need to be alone for the time-being..."

She left the room and closed the door respectfully. Out of respect for both the men in her life, leaving Jules her loving and pained husband standing by the Christmas tree wearing their son's green woollen shirt, staring through the lights into the darkness beyond.

Tomorrow, he would wear his son's red shirt. He always looked good in that one too.

9. Welcome to the Ministry of Defence

"Good Morning Ladies and Gentleman. With your very kind permission of course, I think we'll make a start shall we? We do have rather a lot to get through you will understand. Please, do help yourselves to the refreshments that we have made available here for you today. And may I say that we greatly appreciate you making the journeys from your homes to our modest little office here in London.

Duty Sergeant! Would you please close the door and lock it firmly behind you now? This briefing has now officially begun, starting by the clock on the East Wall at the time of 09.01 am.

I know that you will all understand that for reasons of national security we are unable to tell you our names and positions here inside the Ministry. Suffice to say that we are attached to a particular unit within let's just say The Army for example shall we, and that we are all engaged full time in a very specific project. It's an important project too. You may refer to me as Peter, and the gentleman in the uniform to my left will be Paul. Please do not engage in any kind of conversation with other Ministry staff whilst in the building.

Now, all of you here with us today have one very key thing in common. You have all been informally interviewed, some of you individually and others in panels, over the past few weeks and months. You should know now that you have all been chosen specifically and formally to take part in that same project. As I say we class this as an important project. It's an official one now and congratulations by the way. Your support is highly valued.

For the purpose of reference, we shall refer to it as "Project Spin". You should keep that name to yourselves only. Not to be shared with anyone else. I trust I make myself clear. Her Majesty's Government is really very grateful to you all for agreeing to participate. As you have been informed already, reasonable travel expenses to and from your home or place of work may be claimed for today's visit and the administration officer at the back of the room, that's the tall gentleman in the dark grey suit, white shirt and black tie, will handle that process for you immediately after today's briefing is completed. You may refer to him as Thomas. Please do help yourselves to tea and coffee, it's not the very best in the world I have to say but this is a government department after all!

Now, may I very courteously remind you of the important official documentation that you have all signed voluntarily in order to participate in today's briefing? You are all civilians, as you may already know from chatting earlier as you gathered here in the room today, but you should all take the commitment to secrecy that you have now signed up to really very seriously, jolly seriously indeed. As if you too were in Her Majesty's military service yourselves. Under no circumstances, whatsoever, may you mention your involvement in this project to anyone, not to immediate family friends, neighbours, colleagues at your place of work, local people that you may know, not under any circumstances at all, whatsoever.

If you feel the need to explain to your families your movements from time to time over the next few months, then we recommend that you tell them that you have been invited to take part in some environmental research for the Ministry for the Environment. You can say that your name was chosen at random by a mainframe computer.

We have some paperwork here that we have produced for you today that you may show them in order to help you with that particular activity, and again the administration officer at the back of the room will handle that for you later. For reference, that will be Thomas again.

I know that you will take this need for absolute confidentiality very seriously. In the event that confidentiality is breached in any way, indeed if The Ministry has any reason even to think that it may have been compromised in any way, then you must understand that your involvement in this project will be terminated and with immediate effect. All communication with you will be ended.

It is entirely your decision to continue to take part in this project, and you may leave voluntarily at any point. We would like to comment, however, that due to the rather urgent nature of the project your continued commitment and engagement throughout the rest of the calendar year really would be greatly appreciated by her Majesty's Government. Indeed, your involvement into next calendar year may also be required, potentially, we'll just have to see how it all goes. That's all that we can tell you for the moment. I trust that all makes good and clear sense. And Thankyou again for agreeing to participate.

I shall pause momentarily and ask you if that security explanation is perfectly clear to everyone here today? …. Yes? …..Excellent. We appreciate your attention to this important matter very greatly Ladies and Gentlemen, thank you again on behalf of her Majesty's government.

Today's briefing will be moderately short, at approximately twenty three minutes only. No written notes may be made by you at any point, so please adhere to this important procedure. After that you will all be allowed to leave the building through the same entrance door through which you entered earlier, and to resume your normal daily activities. Are there any questions so far? …. Do please help yourselves to the tea and coffee before it gets cold. It will be cleared away shortly.

By way of a little background you were initially approached individually in order for us to gauge your level of interest in taking part in the said project. You all share a specific common interest. You all have a very active involvement, shall we say, in what we shall just call for the time being the subject of unknown aerial phenomena, more commonly referred to in the popular press as UFOs. This area of commonality will not come as a surprise to any of you in the room this morning, I know. I am not in a position either to confirm or deny the existence of such things here today you will understand. Nor should you ask any of my colleagues here in the room this morning any questions whatsoever on this same subject. That includes all staff present. The official position of Her Majesty's government on this subject is of course very clear, namely that all sightings of so called UFO's may generally be explained by the poor identification of more mundane things such as meteorological phenomena, flocks of birds and weather balloons, bright stars, the planets, aircraft coming in to land, unusual cloud formations, that kind of thing. The Department has never seen the need for any further investigation of this subject as there is no immediate defence threat to the country, nor any direct threat to the citizens of The United Kingdom. We are jolly sure about that.

However, I can confirm now that this topic in general is behind the creation of this project and it is fully appropriate that you are all now aware of this fact here this morning.

You will therefore understand again the need for strict confidentiality given the sensitivity around this controversial subject. Please do be continually mindful of the need for the strictest security, at all times. Questions?

Now, in order to proceed with this briefing, I will need to lay out some possible scenarios to you. You may know that you can ask questions for the purposes of clarification, if you feel the need to, but I may or I may not be in a position to comment or to add further detail. Are there any questions before we move on?

No, well in that case let us move on. We have a great deal to cover.

We live in a huge universe as you all know so well, it is simply huge by any comparison that may be made by man. Far bigger than any of us, with respect, in this small room in the great city of London here today can even begin to imagine. It would indeed be not a little surprising then if the human race was the only form of life, intelligent or otherwise, that has emerged in that same simply huge universe, given its known size.

Are you with me so far? Good. Let's imagine then, just for a moment if we may, that there were indeed other life forms in the universe. Quite a thought I think you will agree. Is everyone comfortable with this concept? It is just a concept at this stage of course, nothing more. All good so far?

Taking this idea further forward a little in that case, with your agreement, let's countenance the idea, just for a few moments if we may, that these other life forms were really rather intelligent. Let us imagine that they had developed the ability to reach far out into different parts of the universe, and to travel very great distances from their planet of origin. Let's take our argument even further forward still, and bravely assume for just a few moments amongst ourselves here this morning, that they had reached the very planet that we live on, that they had reached our Earth. I shall pause here briefly to allow you to consider these intriguing possibilities.

I am asking you therefore here today to countenance the very first scenario of the morning, namely that we are indeed not alone. Which may not be a big shock to you all. Please, do help yourselves to tea and coffee.

This exploration of space by the said species may indeed have been going on for some time. Possibly so. These other life forms may somehow have developed the ability to traverse the huge distances between planets and indeed entire solar systems using propulsion systems that we may only dream of, at our current stage of development. Propulsion systems that are far, far removed from our very mechanical and basic systems of chemical rocket propulsion that use combustible fuels. They may have built quite remarkable systems, remarkable by our primitive standards anyway, that can transport their occupants millions of miles or even billions of miles in a very small amount of time. We are talking distances that would take humans many months and years to cover. A Lifetime in actual fact. Propulsion systems that make man look really very primitive indeed. More of this later. Questions?

In the event that these other beings did indeed exist and that they had reached the planet that we call Earth, this would then be a time of considerable significance for the human race, would it not?

Confirmation of the fact that we are not alone in the universe would be something that many people have dreamed of all of their earthly lives. Indeed, possibly some of you here today may share this very same exciting dream yourselves.

For other groups of people on the other hand, it would simply represent one of the very worst possible nightmares that could befall the inhabitants of this planet. They may hold the view that the arrival of a greatly superior race could only bring grave danger to our society, and even threaten all of mankind. Life would never be the same again, indeed how could life ever find a new normality after such a moment in man's history?

In between these two extremes, there lies another world, one in which governments still have to go about their business and function. I refer here to the governments of major nations such as The United States, Germany, France, Australia, Russia, Canada, China and of course Her Majesty's Government here in Great Britain.

What would the role of national governments be when faced with such a big moment? Would it be to share all of the information with their people that they might have been gathering in secret over the past few decades? Or would it perhaps be to do entirely the opposite and to protect the people from something that was totally new and to some of them, something that was very frightening? To protect them from something that they would best just not know. A justifiable ignorance as it may be referred to. Indeed, just how would the man on the Clapham Omnibus deal with little green men, or grey or whatever colour they might be? You will be more familiar than most people through your extensive reading, and in some illustrious cases here today through your skilled writing on the subject of UFOs, that this scenario offers the very real possibility of an absolute breakdown of our society. One might almost say "Society as we know it, Jim." Pure Chaos is likely to ensue.

Not good. Indeed. Not good at all.

This scenario, the overt and publically confirmed arrival of ET, would surely offer a hugely significant challenge to the leaders of the world's great religions. They might struggle with it. They very probably will, I mean would. They can have made very little preparation to deal with it actually happening. At least that is our understanding.

The structure of security as seen locally through national police forces, and internationally through the armed forces around the world may well find itself under the single greatest threat that it had ever faced, in just one historic moment. A threat that had come out of nowhere, overnight, and very suddenly indeed.

Leaders, Prime Ministers and even Presidents all round the world might be seen immediately by their people as completely powerless. Worse still they could find themselves in an official position of power but without the latest true popular mandate. This is a very dangerous scenario. I am sure you would agree.

"People in nominal power but with no real power on the street". Where it counts most perhaps.

Confidence in the structure of our society would likely crumble. Panic would surely set in almost immediately. Looting would be common. A sense that the end of the world as we have known it had now arrived would surely take hold of many millions of people.

Personal and likely local agendas would grip the population. Remember the broadcast of "The War of the Worlds" by HG Wells, and the panic that was caused amongst our friends in the United States of America when a radio play was taken to be really happening.

Imagine then if you will the task, under these gravest of circumstances, for governments all around the world to hold it all together, a considerable task indeed. Could the loyalty of all of the armed forces even be counted on in such a situation? How would the news first be confirmed to the people? And by whom? Could the world economy possibly survive such an event? What would happen to the distribution of food, of oil and medical supplies? Who would go to work as before? Would there be runs on all of the banks? How long would this situation last? And who would be in control of the planet? Anarchy is a very frightening thing that can take root at an alarming speed. You're seen major riots before, I'm quite certain.

Big questions indeed.

Many are the questions that this scenario forces us to ask, and yet prepare for such a scenario we must.

We live in the Internet Age, where nothing remains secret for very long. Photographs, opinions and ideas are circulated to many people in just a few seconds where once laborious travel by horse was required. Even the speed of a jet airliner is made to seem outdated by the speed of an e-mail, sent with one mouse click to a dozen people in many countries in different time zones, with its multiple attachments. Billions of people use social networks on an hourly basis. In some countries there are more mobile phones in use than there are people that live there. Those nice people from Google have driven past your front door as you slept safely in your bed and taken photographs of your street. We have satellite photographs of the entire planet that we live on and spy satellites can even see the title of a newspaper that a target is reading as he sips his coffee seated at a cafe in the sun, unknowing and many miles below on the surface of the planet. So much is now in what may be referred to as the "Public Domain" and that will not change going forward. Far from it in fact. Indeed, more and more information is being produced and greater amounts of it than ever before are being placed into people's hands. Good but a little dangerous too.

So, how does this relate to the world governments that I spoke about a few moments ago and to the task facing them in the event of the arrival of other entities? Well, some say that it makes their task a great deal easier since the global communication framework across our planet allows vital information to be communicated to their citizens so easily. Procedures, guidance and advice may be sent in just seconds. Situations can be monitored and movements tracked. Continents can communicate with other continents. However, that same public infrastructure has been busy doing something else as well. For many years it has been sharing information across the world with those same people who may be in a state of panic under this scenario. They too have been sharing those photographs, those opinions, and those eyewitness accounts. Their level of knowledge with regard to the existence of other species in the universe has been going up, not down. Specialist interest groups have formed, books have been written and meetings have been held. Views have been expressed, theories put together and experts interviewed. Summaries of notable events have been shared, witnesses presented and technical assessments have been published. They have all been very busy people you see, very busy indeed because it matters to them. It's called Passion.

Questions?

Good…. In short, the people know a lot more than they used to. They are better educated on the subject, receiving their education from each other across the internet and not from the regular teacher as in the normal scenario. They know more, much more, although some things they have not quite properly understood but they are hungry to learn even more.

They should not be underestimated. For the authorities to do so would be a grave error. Their expectations have developed and are on what we might describe as a treadmill. Most significantly, they can take more than they used to be able to, so much more. And this is all hugely significant for those governments around the world, governments trying to cope.

So, Project Spin, your project, what is it and where does it fit into this scenario? Let's imagine that the world governments had decided to share a little more with their people than they had done before. Let's imagine that they had decided to actively release some detail in a drip feed fashion over a period of twelve to eighteen months and that they needed to understand accurately how the people had responded to it. Think of it as a very long version of this briefing that we are all holding here today, but with some simply astounding information deliberately planted within it. How should the government position such information? In what format? And to whom? And when? Who would it confirm as the source of the information and who could the people go to if they had further questions, which they surely would? Where would the media fit into this and what would the goal be? Let's not forget that as our American friends say "Once the toothpaste is out of the tube, you ain't going to get it back in!" Indeed. For a process would be underway, an unstoppable one at that. Clear so far?

So, perhaps a focus group would be a good place to start. A small group of people who could gather every month or two let's say in a government building such as this and discuss some ideas about how this news might be marketed to the people. A group of intelligent people with an above average level of interest in the subject, people from many walks of life, people like you. To discuss how the story might best be spun.

Hence "Project Spin."

Ah, here comes the officer to take the tea and coffee away, thankyou. Are there any clarification questions at this point? No? Very good, let's move forward to the next scenario then shall we?

Let us now consider that there was to be an impending moment facing the people of Planet Earth that the governments of the world had come to know of. This was to be big. Perhaps this news had been deliberately communicated to them by the superior race so that they might respond and prepare their people well for that important day. Let us imagine that this event was highly significant and was to happen within a timeframe of just five years' time.

World governments would have a choice to respond or not. For the purposes of today, let us work to the second of those scenarios, namely that the governments do indeed choose to respond. They need to prepare their peoples for something that the majority of their people would surely never even have considered, let alone been prepared for in any way at all.

A process of specifically drip feeding ideas, concepts and past experiences would need to be put into place immediately in order that the peoples of planet Earth could become very familiar with some basic cosmic ideas. These would be ideas that relate to our being one of many life forms in the universe, that we are not particularly high up the cosmic pecking order either, and most importantly of all that the notion of a human-centred universe created by a very tall omnipotent white man with a beard and a white robe was not an entirely accurate description of what has been going on all around us, over a very long time indeed.

This would be a process that would have to communicate ideas that I know you will be more than familiar with. Ideas that might include, amongst others, things like, ooh I don't know, maybe....

Roswell, New Mexico...

Rendlesham Forest here in the UK ...

Shag Harbour, Newfoundland ...

Vaghina in Brasil ...

The closing down of over ten MinuteMan Intercontinental Ballistic Missiles at major US installations by UFOs flying overhead ..

... and on other Military bases too...

US Aircraft carriers being visited at sea by strange lights...

Apollo space craft having company on all of their flights into space...

Strange vehicles parked by the crater on the Moon – and simply gigantic ones too.

Moments like a former American President meeting secretly with the leader of the superior race at an American air force base way back in the late 50s – not then at the dentist as was the public cover story of the time.

Of captured space craft and of technology that has indeed been reverse-engineered

Of the weaponisation of space...

Of potential environmental disaster, and yes at our own hands...

And of the human race taking its place at the inter-stellar table in an informed and responsible way...

That kind of thing. Clear so far?

Questions?

And you fit in where? We thought that you might be able to help us understand how these ideas could best be communicated to hundreds of millions of people all around the world in a short space of time, without that catastrophic breakdown in the world order happening as we all fear it might. Likely will by all assessments.

All rather important stuff you see.

Is this something that you think you could help us with? In order to begin, we thought that we would divide you into groups of six people per table to consider some of the larger Challenges and Issues ahead.

Any questions?

No?

Excellent, then let us begin our important work here today …

10. You Lucky Git!

It was only six forty in the morning, but Larry's day already seemed to be going very well, very well indeed thank you very much. He had woken up naturally at six am about a minute before his Samsung Galaxy alarm clock was due to go off. He knew from recent experience that his day always went so much better when he had woken up naturally on his own, without the aid of mechanical help such as an artificial alarm. And today was such a fortunate day. This was definitely a good start to his day!

As he lay there in bed thinking ahead to the day stretching out before him, he reached over to get his phone and to turn off the alarm thus saving himself from hearing the harsh morning sound that he generally wanted it to make most mornings in order to wake him up. The little red marker was showing on his device to indicate that there were some messages waiting for him and so he sat up a little more in bed. He would flick through the important ones very briefly, before getting up to shave and shower. He switched the bedside light on in order to see better.

Good news, that busy little "Canadian pharmacy" was it doing its thing again, that thing that it did so well all around the world with a really hard resolve, namely attempting to sell Viagra tablets at an amazing discount better than you could find anywhere else! He made a mental note to take another look at the e-mail later in the day in the event that he felt his regular Viagra supplier was… flagging in some way, flagging commercially that is. There were also three lovely Russian girls apparently really exciting ones too, who wanted personally to meet him, and to provide him with continuous physical pleasure whenever he desired this, and all he had to do was to call this number and ask for "Irena". Ah yes, the lovely Irena, he wondered how she was doing this lovely spring morning, or rather should that be "who" she was doing? Probably no need to bring the Canadian pharmacy's Viagra along then to a rendezvous with the lovely Irena, even if the discount was the best that you could hope to find anywhere. Just no need for Viagra at all you see, not with the gorgeous Irena.

Then there was a really interesting e-mail from his boss sent for some reason at 1.13 am. Not only had his annual pay rise just been successfully approved, but she had also managed to get it back dated three months, and as if that wasn't good enough news that new amount would all be recognised fully in his next pay packet. She, Laura his manager, estimated that this was worth to him a little over £1,125 pounds, after Tax, and he was to be congratulated for having done such a good job over the preceding twelve month period. He deserved his rise fully she said and his hard work had caught the attention of the firm's ambitious new Managing Director. No need for the Viagra at work either then he thought to himself!

Oh, and one other good thing, he was getting another five thousand shares in the company in recognition of his achievement, and they could vest over two years now and not the four year period as was the case before. That way he could get his hands on the money twice as quickly as he was legally allowed to before, that was assuming that the company's share value continued to rise like it had been recently. It had taken quite a dip of around twenty one per cent suddenly last week on the back of a competitor's new product announcement and subsequent launch.

This was probably the very week when his new shares would have been allocated to him at that lower price, so he had probably already made something like a twenty per cent gain on his new company stock in just a few weeks. Oh good, he thought, that lovely little silver convertible gets closer and closer...!

As if all that wasn't good enough to get his day off to a positive start, a lovely man over in Nigeria called Mr Rainbow of Rainbow Legal Associates had some even better news for him. This was news that was meant just for him personally, according to this very nice and helpful man in a faraway continent. One of Larry's long lost uncles who had moved to the lovely warm country of Nigeria a number of years ago in order to escape the great cold of the British winter, had sadly passed away quite recently. Oh no, how very sad thought Larry, trying to recall the uncle in question with a little difficulty.

Mr Rainbow unfortunately didn't have the exact date of death of the uncle to hand but he felt sure that it was definitely quite recently. Anyway, the positive news was that a very large sum of money had been left in his uncle's last and official will which had just been read out in the local crown court, and would you believe it, but Larry had all of the money from his uncle left just for him?! There was over a million pounds in total, apparently, plus some land and property and some original art work too. Gosh, what an interesting package, it just goes to show that there is indeed light at the end of the rainbow sometimes.

It was all there in black and white in his uncle's will! How amazing! In order to receive the money, all Larry now had to do was to send the friendly Mr Rainbow his address, his bank and national insurance details, bank password details "would be helpful" too, and the money would come through into his account the following day. It was as simple as that, apparently! Oh, and if you could include your full home address just for security purposes please, and details of any other bank or savings accounts that he had, that would be "very helpful". He looked forward to hearing back from Larry soon. Yes, I'm sure it would be helpful, thought Larry, helpful to you mate but not to me! A nice pot of gold for you at the end of the rainbow if I send you all of my personal data my new friend, - I think not!

"Delete" was pressed.

Finally, and more importantly, there was a brilliant text from a lovely lady that he had met at a business fair over in Zurich recently, saying that she would be over in London next Thursday and yes she should be delighted to meet him for dinner this time, adding that she was sorry that she had only time for a few drinks last time that they had met at that fair. If "things got on top of" her she might have to stay the entire weekend and catch the later Sunday evening flight back home. The text ended with a "x", how very encouraging thought the lucky Larry. What an interesting start to the day he was having! A pay rise from the boss, a backdated pay rise too in his next pay cheque, more shares given to him, people contacting him in his morning bed from both Russia and Africa, a good result on a hot date, and he hadn't even put the Philips kettle on yet to make his first cup of tea!

With a good spring in his step already so early in the day, and for so many different reasons, he jumped out of bed, completely forgetting the very badly swollen ankle he had got the previous evening when out running. Instead of landing on his right foot and immediately feeling great pain, there was just a very dull ache, really not too bad, and nothing more. It really wasn't that uncomfortable, it seemed to have pretty well healed itself overnight just through having the weight taken off it while he slept. He felt confident that he would be able to go out and do a good run after a couple of days or so of rest too. Good news! He walked across to the flat's kitchen and turned on that lovely futuristic Philips kettle of his, made in a pristine white plastic. He had won it luckily the weekend before in a local raffle, together with a case of lovely Argentinian red wine, and this was the first time that he was going to use it to make a brew. He had let it stand overnight with cold tap water in it to be sure that it was completely clean inside. So he now emptied that stale water out, and filled it half full and switched her on. She whirred into life instantly, and within a minute there was good boiling hot water ready for a cuppa. This will save me time in the mornings he thought, so much faster than his old kettle, how very helpful. As he opened the cupboard door there was his favourite mug right in front of him, now what were the chances of that occurring he thought? There are seven mugs in my cupboard, so there's a one in seven chance of my favourite red Friday mug being right there in front of me and there it was today, just when he needed it! Two minutes later he was on his way into the bathroom with a piping hot cup of tea in his hand and in the best coloured mug of the seven in his weekly collection. This was just perfect for a Friday morning!

Larry took out a new razor once a month, and today was the big day for that little monthly ceremony to be performed. He opened up a Brut brown and green striped zip-up toiletry bag that he kept his bathroom things in but dropped it by mistake on the floor. Careless Larry, but when he had picked it up and unzipped it, there on top was the exact new green razor that he had wanted to take out. That saved him from having to rummage around inside the bag to find the right razor, which always took time and in addition ran the risk of him perhaps cutting his hand on something sharp inside. He applied the fragrant shave gel to his stubble with great energy and a very manly performance generally, and then slowed right down to begin shaving with the sharp new blade. He was always very careful to shave slowly with a new blade, for fear of it cutting him deeply, and so he took his time, even taking a little tea break halfway through the task, drinking from his preferred red Friday mug.

In the background, he could just hear on the radio that he had switched on walking into the bedroom the news that his team had just been drawn in the next round of the FA Cup to play the great Manchester United! Imagine that, our little local team playing with the big boys, and even better the announcer confirmed that the first leg would be at their home ground. That would bring in much needed revenue to their local club, and the welcome income from that one match alone would enable them to upgrade the player's dressing room, to finish off the fan's new cafe and bar area, and in addition maybe even to build their new website. All from one match! Great news, "that's a result" thought Larry, all the lads will be dead pleased with that news! We'll have a few beers tonight to celebrate. What a morning …

He returned to the shaving task in hand but this time Larry was a little over confident with his shaving technique and thought that he had just run the new razor far too close to his chin for comfort and had suddenly cut into it quite deeply. There was then that difficult ten seconds or so that every man who shaves will be very familiar with when you think you've cut yourself, and you wait anxiously to see if the cut appears on your face in the mirror, and the blood starts to gush out for what seems like an eternity. He got to five and then eight and then the full ten seconds, and there was no sign of the cut opening up. No blood at all now either. Phew! He gently touched the affected area on his chin with the pad of his forefinger, it felt a little tender but there didn't appear to be any break in his skin and to his great relief no blood came out when he pushed a little harder.

In fact, when he then touched it even harder still, not only was there definitely no cut nor any red blood showing, but he discovered that he had just achieved the perfect shave! Now you're talking he thought, and so he emptied the water in his post-perfect shave sink and jumped into his spectacular manly power shower, cast in silver aluminium. The water came out good and hot right away, there was a good flow too. He had got his shampoo ready, which he had bought the day before in a special two for the price of one offer, "available for a limited period only". Lucky Larry liked a real bargain you see.

He had woken up that night with quite a painful right eye, and he had known that he had something going round in the eye for a few days but he had not been able to get it out successfully. He had got up in the night to try to flush the object out with some warm water from the hot tap but it hadn't worked and he had returned to his bed with a sore eye. As he was in the shower he thought he would stick his head under the water, facing upwards, and open up his right eye ever so slightly to see if the jets of water might dislodge whatever was causing the irritation. Something did seem momentarily to shift position under the top eyelid and he leaned out of the powerful flow and placed his finger very gently into his eye to see if anything came out. Yes! Sure enough, a very black eyelash came out of his eye and onto the surface of his middle finger and it was a large one too. Another good result! That felt so much better already and his idea had worked brilliantly. He did the same with the other eye, since he was already in the relevant position in the shower, and then placed his finger precisely into that eye too just in case there was a foreign body in that one as well, but he certainly wasn't expecting to find anything there. To his surprise, there had been two eyelashes in that eye as well, and big ones again at that! He washed them away quickly under the shower and went on with the rest of his showering.

By now the man's face felt wonderfully smooth, he could see properly out of both clean eyes, and he would look good for the rest of the day now for sure. Teeth were cleaned, and a free £1 voucher was found in the toothpaste packet "Redeemable at any branch of Boots" in the next three months it read. That'll do nicely he said, as he admired his oh so smooth face and dazzlingly white teeth in the matching aluminium bathroom mirror. At that very moment, something caught his eye just slightly in the wall mirror, something was poking out from behind the cabinet behind him. He turned round and picked up a small slip of paper, which turned out to be a national lottery ticket. He had bought it a few weeks back and had then lost it, or so he thought, but here it was safe but a little damp now from the bathroom steam. He went into the kitchen and quickly ironed the ticket dry in one very impressive right-handed swish of the silver chrome steam iron.

This was the steam iron model by the way that had packed up just two days before the three year guarantee was due to expire. Having found the original receipt carefully put away for just this potential tragic "white goods moment", he had been given an upgraded version of this model in his local hardware shop the weekend before completely free of charge, and with a new five year guarantee this time on this latest model as well!

He would take his now crisply ironed dry lottery ticket out to work with him and get it checked out somewhere, for you never know, "It could be you!" as they said in the National Lottery ads on the telly. So he tucked the ticket carefully into the back pocket of his new Ben Sherman jeans. He patted the pocket twice, just for good luck you understand.

As he was leaving the flat, the daily post was delivered a little earlier than usual, and so for some reason he decided to open it quickly before heading out to the world of work. There was the usual junk mail with "buy one get one pizza free" offers from Mr Domino, several business cards for the local taxi cab firm and a flyer from "Chris, your friendly professional tree surgeon". He opened a very boring old brown envelope from the Electricity company and looked at the statement inside just briefly. Good news, the company's computer had made a calculation error with its last quarterly statement for his property, and they could now confirm that he was to be credited with £229.78p later that same month. As part of the energy firm's "progressive new Customer Charter" following their recent acquisition by an efficient and clearly very switched-on German utilities group, a goodwill gesture of an additional £75 would also be credited to his account that same month for their unintended computing billing error. They wished to apologise for their error on his account too. They thanked him for his ongoing domestic fuel business and hoped that he had not been too inconvenienced by their mistake. He thanked them back, he had not been through any inconvenience, and he liked these things called "Customer Charters", whatever their country of origin. This kind of post he liked.

The front door closed behind him and he walked over to his car.

The traffic seemed very light this morning, and even the road works that had been causing so much delay for the past two weeks were being wrapped up and the contra flow arrangement was being dismantled. The traffic lights were still just in place though and his was the last vehicle to go through the green light before the dreaded four to five minute wait! So famous was this traffic delay locally that the local paper had run a feature on it under the title of "Road works – oh no it doesn't!" Anyway, his vehicle was nicely through now and making good progress. There was just enough time for him to stop by the newsagent on the way into work, and would you believe it, but there was someone just leaving a parking space right outside the shop's front door. Perfect! The car was a little green Mazda convertible with a very pretty dark-haired girl behind the wheel, and she flashed her lights at him to thank him for waiting a little to let her out. He did the same, and unbelievably she did the same back, waving and smiling at him as she sped away onto the main road. He thought that he recognised her vaguely from somewhere, perhaps the local pub or a local party perhaps?

He parked in what had just been her space and as he got out of his car, there on the ground, was a crisp new £50 note just laying on the tarmac, fresh out of the cash machine probably. It must have belonged to the pretty girl in the green Mazda and he turned round to see if he could still see her and catch her attention somehow, but she was well on her way down the road now. He put the new banknote in his breast pocket and hoped that he just might see her again somehow one day soon. You never know ...

Martin the newsagent knew Larry well, and greeted him with "Hello mate, you doing all right? How's those blooming road works down the road then?!"

"Well, I think they may finally be finishing them as we speak, I just flew through!"

"Blimey, God must like you today then mate. I've heard no end of stories about people being delayed there for ages. One bloke in a van said that he was even going to do the repairs himself and that he'd get the job done quicker that way!"

"Don't blame him mate, it's a bloody disgrace. Welcome to Britain and all that! I'll have my usual newspaper and mag Martin, and I'm feeling lucky so give me a Euro millions ticket will you? Oh, and can you check this old lottery ticket for me, found it this morning tucked away in a corner in the bathroom! I don't want a million quid thanks that would just be too greedy wouldn't it? A hundred grand would be just fine, thank you my friend! Cash would be fine!"

Martin got the usual paper and science magazine for him, and then ran Larry's newly found ironed ticket through the machine. He then went very quiet and looked across at his regular customer. For once, the jovial Martin looked ever so serious.

Another customer came into the shop at that point and browsed the magazines behind him. Martin leaned over, called Larry a little closer and broke into a very serious whisper.

"Mate, straight up all right? No bullshit. Twenty one grand".

Larry was looking at the front page of the paper and replied:

"Yeah, whatever, that would be very acceptable too. You could do some real damage with that kind of money that's for sure!"

Martin took the newspaper from Larry's hand very firmly, looked across at the other customer, smiled at her and then Martin looked Larry squarely in the face again, and very deliberately.

"Mate, it is you, that's what I'm trying to say, the machine just told me that you've won twenty one grand. No bull, here look at the slip of paper it's just printed off. You lucky git!"

Larry still thought Martin was pulling his plonker, and told him to try much harder and this time to sound as though he actually meant it. Martin shoved the piece of paper directly into his face and told him to read it whilst he politely but quickly served the other customer. When she had left the shop a few moments later, Larry began to see that it was actually true. He really had won that amount of money like Martin was telling him and there was a Winning Ticket hotline that he now needed to call and they would arrange to deliver the money safely to him at a time and place of his choice, which could be in cash or by cheque, or both if he wished. The final words on the slip of paper read :

"You see, we said it could be you!" And it was.

Flipping heck, this was turning out to be some Friday, and he hadn't even got to work yet! Martin shook Larry's hand and congratulated him on his wonderful win. He had always wanted this to happen with one of his regulars, and the largest ever amount that had been won in his shop was just £250, and he had to give the customer this amount in cash from the till. But the larger amounts automatically get the National Lottery head office involved, like this one did for lucky Larry.

"Here, I'm feeling lucky mate, I could be on a roll here, let's do the Euro Millions scratch card shall we too now then?" Martin passed him a card. Larry leaned over the counter, as two school children came into the shop to buy some sweets, and worked their way round the entire counter to make sure that they were getting the best possible value. Larry suddenly squealed with excitement, giggled loudly, and then winked at the two boys. Now who was being a kid, eh?

"No Mate, you haven't, have you?! Martin enquired. "Blimey, you have haven't you? You jammy git, you've got lucky again haven't you? How much this time? he asked as he served the two lads.

Hearing this exclusive unfolding drama they weren't going to go away until they'd got their answer, and they joined in the men's conversation.

"Mister, what have you won then? Are you a millionaire then? I've never met a millionaire".

"Well lads, if you get four of the same thing under the scratch card, then you get £400. Pretty good, yes? But if you choose wisely where to scratch and manage to get five that are all the same, like I just did here, then you win £2,000. Look, five beautiful gold keys all the same, that's £2,000 to me, thank you very much, yes indeed, in the bank!"

"Blimey, mate, God really must like you all right! You jammy bugger, whatever you have for breakfast each morning, I'm having the same thing from now on. And I'm changing my aftershave and all!"

"You've either got it mate, or you don't got it! And today, it looks like I got it! I'll come back and take you out for a curry one night next week, and you can help me count my cash on the table how's that?" said Larry. That would be Lucky Larry then.

Just then the door opened, and who should make a re-appearance but the sexy lady with the Mazda convertible. She was very well dressed, and walked over to the counter and said in a very lovely French accent:

"Gentlemen, Bonjour, I wonder if perhaps you may help me? Just the few minutes ago, I am having lost some English money when I was mounting my car. Is it possible maybe that my money has been found by someone nearby and had been brought in to you personally?"

Lucky Larry stepped in here, and in his best French introduced himself, explained that he thought that he could help here, and magically produced a £50 note that he had just found outside on the floor, a note produced from his breast pocket, where else? A huge smile appeared on the lovely young lady's beautiful French face and she looked very relieved.

"Oh, monsieur, vous etes tres gentil, merci beaucoup"....

(Stage direction here - slight pause and a change in language from French back into English, accompanied by a slightly naughty expression) ..

..."perhaps I may reward you for monsieur for your great kindness, maybe there is a lovely English pub nearby to here where I can buy you lunch later today?", her delicate French hand momentarily touching his manly English arm.

And Larry thought that Christmas only happened in December!

Larry somehow thought that he could just about fit this delightful invitation into his schedule that day, and so he swapped mobile phone numbers with the lovely Agnes, and explained that The Queen's Head about two miles down the road was really rather lovely. He thought that they would have an enjoyable lunch down there for sure, and he looked forward to luncheon very much, how very decadent!

One hell of a Friday this was turning out to be! Oh, one other thing, would he mind if her sister Chantelle joined them too? No, that should be fine, confirmed Lucky Larry swallowing nervously, he thought that he could fit that in. The lovely Agnes giggled at this last idea, looked at him in a teasing kind of way that women can do so well, and waived "A bientot" to the two men, her beautiful French form slipping out in the early morning air, leaving tantalising traces of perfume hanging in the air. God Bless the European Union, he thought. That's why he had voted to stay in then!

Larry thanked Martin for his company, and for his excellent service, and told him to put Thursday night in the diary for their celebration curry together. With that, he headed out to his car and off to work. A young man was standing by his car apparently cleaning all of the windows, how very strange!

"Can I help you mate?" Larry asked him.

"Just doing your windows sir, like you asked, that's three quid please!"

"Not me mate, you've got your wires crossed. Look there's the same model of car as mine in the same colour over there, you're doing the wrong car mate!"

"Oh yeah, right, well on the house it is then mate, it's your lucky day. Have a nice day".

And so the very fortunate Larry drove to work that memorable spring morning, two thousand pounds wealthier, with a hot date, or was that two hot dates coming up at lunchtime down at the Queens Head, a pay rise behind him, that's a backdated pay rise, thousands of more shares in the company, and the choice of a further twenty one grand in cash, cheque or a mixture of both, still to be delivered to him at home, or at work, or wherever he wanted it, and at a time of his choosing.

And all this in a car with the windows as clean as clean could be. Things certainly looked bright for the lucky Larry. The weekend ahead was looking good! What had this man done to deserve all of this Good Fortune?

After all, they say you make your Own Luck now, don't they?

11. Spiritual Roadside Assistance

"Thank you very much indeed, sir. I have now successfully taken note here in my rescue van of the precise geographical location of both you and your vehicle. And would you perhaps happen to kindly know the very precise postal code of the hotel premises where your vehicle is now located Mr Hill, please Sir?"

There was something almost hypnotic about the voice of the AA man. He sounded fully confident that he would get to you quickly, which was what a stranded motorist needs most, but there was a little more to his voice than just … plain confidence. He sounded like a robot!

"Er, now you're asking! I don't think I do I'm afraid, but it's in the Ascot area so it will be something like SL5 or something similar, will that help you a little?.

"That's really quite all right Mr Hill, rest assured, I will definitely be able to find it here on the fully reliable satellite navigation system here in my modern van vehicle. That will be fine I'm sure, totally, one hundred percent fine, and thankyou. We will get you sorted and back out on the open road again in your transportation vehicle really very quickly, before you even know it. In a jiffy in fact, yes indeed, Sir".

There it was again, that confidence thing coming through in his voice. But it was more than that wasn't it, there was another quality of some kind that lay deep within his voice. It was something rather lovely to connect with but also quite difficult to describe. Certainly calm and quite reassuring. It was a rather amazing way of communicating with another person, but Mr Hill couldn't quite find the right adjective to describe it, confident yes, strong certainly, powerful too, but quietly and firmly so. Somehow like he knew something that we didn't, in some way. Whatever in the world that could possibly be! Interesting too but something like a robot about it ….

This humble AA man possessed a confident, strong, quiet power deep inside him then. Not bad for a grubby guy driving around in a bright yellow van, thought the stranded Mr Hill.

"Ah yes of course, you guys have all the technology now these days don't you?" he said back.

"Well yes we do sir, in its own modest human way. I'm not sure though that it provides solutions to all of mankind's current issues on your troubled planet but yes it certainly helps to get us to our stranded vehicular Customers that little bit quicker. Which can't be a bad thing… mate, right?"

And again! This time though he sounded just slightly metallic in his tone, particularly with that last phrase with the word "mate" slipped in, it sounded a little prepared and cold too. "Mate" seemed a very odd choice of word, incongruous, and quite false. But again his voice seemed to wash over you somehow and to warm you with all of its strong reassurance. It was all a little strange, even unnerving, like he knew something really significant that you didn't yet know, and we're not talking here about something low-level like the internal wiring diagram of comfortable French hatchback. There was almost a tangible warm glow coming to you from his words, and that was just from speaking with him on the phone! It was curious, even slightly spooky.

Mr Hill shook himself out of these silly thoughts, telling himself that it's just an AA guy that you're talking to here. Must be a bad line that's giving you all of these daft impressions and that funny tone of his on the phone, he concluded. Yes, that would be it.

"If you do get lost, just give me a call on this same number please that you just called me on and I'm sure I can guide you in. It's a pretty big hotel on your left-hand side as you're approaching from the London Road. As they say "you can't miss it!"

"Very good Mr Hill, you are an excellent person, thank you for your latest offer of help. I shall travel in this vehicle to you just as soon as I am able. So just to confirm our current conversation, that's a Citroen Xantia hatchback, with a three litre petrol combustion engine, in black, your vehicle is automatic, she's on an S plate, cool car aby, very well polished, and she's parked in the lower part of the hotel's car park one foot away from the small wooden fence and currently with no vehicle on either side of it or in front."

How did he know these last few details, wondered Mr Hill? He hadn't even mentioned to him how the car was parked. Spooky.

"Yes, that's correct. I will be with my car, and you should see it parked on your right as you come down through the car park".

"Actually Sir, I shall enter in such a way that you and your vehicle will both be on my left. Thank you so much indeed. Your front driver's side tyre is possibly five pounds light in pressure."

"Oh really, is that so? You sound remarkably confident about that!"

No comment came back.

"One other thing Sir, Mr Hill please, thank you in advance, would you by any chance have such a thing as a photographic image of your vehicle that you could kindly send me, you excellent person?"

"Pardon?"

"I have just said, do you have such a thing as a photographic image of your vehicle car that you could send me across the air, please Mr Hill, you excellent person?"

"You want me to send you a photograph of my car, is that what you're asking me?"

"That is completely correct Sir", he replied so darned well. That big confidence thing was there again. Mr Hill so wished that he could speak just like this man did, it was amazing to listen to, captivating, reassuring and slightly controlling.

"Well, yes I do have several photographs of my car on my phone actually. May I ask you why that matters?"

"It just helps me actually to do a better job for you Sir, when I get to you very shortly, before you even know it Mr Hill. Yes, indeed, for you, and thank you".

"I'll do it right away now then, see you soon hopefully. Bye for now".

Mr Hill sent a photo through to the AA man's phone straight away, although it was an unusually long phone number that he had with over twenty digits and characters included in there too. He had never ever seen a number quite like it, most unusual. Exactly which intergalactic network does that come from, he wondered?!

Ten seconds later, his phone rang again.

"Feel free to put the bonnet down now if you'd like to sir. One of the rubber material tyres is a little low on your car Mr Hill excellent person, you might want to take a look at that soon, next time you go past a fossil fuel garage with a silver and black tyre pressure machine, Sir. That's the front nearside tyre sir as you may call it, oh and you have only two tyre valve caps present on your vehicle sir. You might want to purchase a little packet of four tyre valve caps when you go in to that same fossil fuel garage to pump your tyre up, sir, thank you indeed. Ones that have been carefully fashioned from metal materials have greater durability than your plastic material."

Bloody hell, this was amazing! Some service he was getting from the AA today! He looked down at the tyre and the AA man was absolutely right, one of the tyres was visibly low. Then he rapidly worked out what was happening of course - he was being tricked surely, and probably being filmed too on a hidden camera positioned somewhere high up in a tree in the hotel's car park, right? That was it! He looked around the car park, thinking that the AA man had already arrived and was winding him up in some way by talking to him on the phone from his parked vehicle just a few yards away. He just hadn't heard his electric vehicle pull up quietly and park, that was all. Yes, that would be the simple explanation.

But no, there was no bright yellow rescue vehicle anywhere to be seen. Nor one of any other colour in fact. His was the only car in that area in fact, and he suddenly felt a little vulnerable. He wanted to be on his way and out of this eerie car park soon. It was colder now too, much colder suddenly.

"So, I shall be with you very soon Sir, very soon indeed, excellent person".

"I'm sorry, what did you say your name was again?"

"My name is John, Mr Hill, only plain John, thank you indeed, Sir."

This man was anything but plain. And this prank was starting to get to him now.

"And have you been with the AA a long time, you seem to know some impressive things about my vehicle before you've even got to me?!"

"Oh yes Sir, I have been in this business for a very long time indeed, many good years in fact, a period of time far greater that you can possibly imagine. You are in good experienced hands with me Mr Hill, please. See you shortly in my yellow emergency rescue vehicle van car, with an AA logo on the side of it…"

…and he rang off. Abruptly.

Mr Hill walked up the slope of the hotel car park just a few brief yards, in that way that only a stranded motorist can, hands behind his back, pacing slowly and looking down at the ground for no particular reason, glancing at his watch to record the time of his last phone call with the AA man so that he could estimate when he would get there, in about an hour's time. He so wanted to be on his way by now, and get this all over and done with.

"Good morning Mr Hill, how very nice to meet you, excellent person".

He turned round as fast as the hotel car park's soft pine-cone covered ground would let him, and there he was! One very real AA man standing right there now, and one very bright yellow emergency rescue vehicle right behind him too, with its busy flashing lights going around on the top of the cabin, but with the van strangely making absolutely no noise at all. Just how in the name of someone's God had he done that?! There had been no noise coming from the vehicle approaching up the road or from it parking up, he hadn't heard the truck's door open and close as someone climbed out, and besides they had only just ended their last phone call about ten seconds ago. And yet here was this mysterious AA man right before him now, as large as life, the confident voice on the phone come to life right in front of him in an impossibly fast time! And he was unnaturally tall too …!

Wow!

"Hi, I wasn't expecting you that quickly" he garbled.

"All part of the service Mr Hill, we aim to please and to be very human".

That damned confidence thing in his voice again. But strangely metallic too, as before.

He looked at the man and found that he couldn't look away. He was drawn to him, and particularly drawn into his attractive but very dark green eyes. John was really tall, probably nearer to seven feet tall than six foot, and with enormous black boots on his feet but both were unlaced. The two men stood there for quite some time with no words being spoken, and he thought that he could feel a warmth coming from the AA man, literally a physical warmth emanating from him. He was a very tall man indeed, and he just stood there really well, filling the space with his giant body, and so perfectly, perfectly still. No swaying at all. Neither to the side, nor backward or forward, just rooted to the spot in some way.

This was someone with a great presence.

Another thing, the birds had stopped singing, and all was quiet around the car park very suddenly. No other sounds …

He smiled at Mr Hill, and said nothing. Or rather he said nothing in the normal way that we do with the mouth and words. His dark green eyes, or were they actually black now, seemed to be speaking to him, saying good reassuring things.

Then he spoke out aloud, the old-fashioned human way of speaking.

"You're car is fine now Mr Hill, sir. There was a small electrical problem with power not getting through from what you call the battery to what you call the starter motor. But it is completely fine now and it will all work strongly for you, from now on. Yes. You can get to your beautiful daughter's birthday party on time now Mr Hill. Oh, and she will be delighted with the puppy you've brought her, that was very thoughtful of you.

She has a particular name in her mind that she's been thinking of for some time now, ever since you and your lovely dark-haired wife Sarah mentioned to her that you might get her a puppy for her birthday".

Mr Hill stood speechless.

How? What? How?

Who was this man?

How could he humanly know these things?

"Oh, and don't worry about that little health issue that your doctor was talking to you about in her surgery last Thursday morning at 11.20 am. You've been worrying about it a lot recently, but it will soon resolve itself and you will be fully recovered inside the period that you call one calendar month. Indeed. Confirmed. Please try your vehicle now Mr Hill, excellent person, I'll just get back into my emergency rescue vehicle and write up the physical paperwork for you with a pen that has been filled with black ink."

He watched the unnaturally tall John return to the still silent emergency rescue vehicle, both orange lights still going round on top, and get into the driver's cab to do his paperwork. He thought that he could see a black suit, with a white shirt and black tie hanging up behind him inside the cab on a brown wooden coat hanger. That was odd, for an AA man. And now he was wearing sunglasses inside the cab of his van. He wasn't before.

Mr Hill then got back onto his own vehicle and started the engine, suddenly realising that he had just seen the visitor somehow nearly float up into the driver's cab instead of climbing up as you would expect. This was getting stranger by the moment. He reached over to the glove box to check that his wallet was there, he wanted to give the amazing John some money to thank him for fixing his car, and so fast.

As he leaned back into his seat with his wallet in his left hand, he looked into his rear view mirror momentarily. John the tall AA man and his bright yellow emergency rescue vehicle were nowhere to be seen. They had made no noise, he had not said goodbye nor had he asked Mr Hill to sign any kind of paperwork.

Two minutes later and Mr Hill was in his car and turning out of the hotel's car park. At the junction, he opened his window to be sure to cross over carefully as the light was fading. As he did so, he was struck by the sound of the birds singing away loudly. Just a few minutes ago they had been utterly silent. And there up the road signalling to turn into the same hotel car park, was a bright yellow AA van. This was a regular noisy diesel van that you could hear coming down the road from a hundred yards away and so it turned into the main entrance.

As he pulled out of the hotel slip road, he thought he caught sight of a very tall man on the other side of the road, standing back in the shadows under the long branches of the pine trees. It looked like it was a man wearing a black suit, with a white shirt and a black tie on, and he was standing still, but really still, simply watching. Like he was rooted to the spot somehow. Very strange, why would anyone stand there? And what was there to watch? There was no reason to do that. Also he thought he saw that the man had sunglasses on as well, just like those that John had been wearing….

12. Jack and Me

Dearest Jack,

When we talk my son, I need you to look at me, in the eye, and directly into my face. Do you think that you could do that for me?

Please.

You are happy to talk with me but you seem to do it whilst you're looking at the screen on your mobile phone, or your ipad, or your laptop, or on your play station thing, or on the television screen. Sometimes more than one of them at the same time. It drives me nuts, Jack. Honestly it does.

You don't get it though, I know.

If you're going to cook a meal for all of us in the evening, that's wonderful. You do a pretty good chicken stir-fry as you know. But would you please mind washing your hands first? Not like you do in three seconds when I've told you to wash them, but by taking your time and using some soap or something similar and really washing them properly. Out of respect for us all.

Thank you - from us all.

When your lovely funny mates with their facial stubble come round to pick you up in the winter in their funny vehicles to go to the pub or to the cinema or somewhere, do you think that you and they could possibly walk round to our front door on the concrete path thing? That is what it's there for you see. Paths are for walking on, they get you to where you need to go, they do lead somewhere I promise you my son. If they all walk directly across the wet grass you see it makes the state of our grass even worse, and it brings mud into our hallway unnecessarily and in addition your lovely brand new £80 trainers soon get dirty that way too. I would very much like the postman to be aware of this concrete path option too but he's not my son you see, and he doesn't live here, so we haven't had this conversation yet.

Thank you in advance for using our concrete path from now on, and particularly in the winter.

Back to the house, when you've taken something out of a cupboard, it will definitely need to go back at some point, ideally into the same cupboard whence it came. Do you even know the word "whence" Jack?

And read more, like we do. It's good for you, you'll learn new words like eclectic, variegated and whence. Books, have you heard of them? They're classics really.

For god's sake, if you're going to wear shoes with laces, undo them when you put your shoes on. If you don't like that, then buy slip-ons. Just look at what you're doing to the heels of your brand new black work shoes, forcing your feet in to them with the laces still tied in a bow, shoes that we bought for you three weeks ago at the absurd price of £70!

Undo your shoelaces first, please son. Or buy slip-ons.

Jack, now this is what we call a bedroom cupboard. You see all of your clothes on the floor down there strewn liberally throughout your bedroom, well they go in here, up here into the cupboard, actually right inside it beyond the two open doors. The door then closes, no not on its own, you need to close it like this let me demonstrate. There, see? That way, all of your favourite clothes are inside the same bedroom cupboard and where you can easily find them the next time that you need them, the bedroom floor is clear and it can also be cleaned with a device that we call a hoover. And yes you can then stick your stickers and posters on the outside of cupboard door, okay?

Happy now? Repeat after me "bedroom cupboard".

Please, please, please, could you find a little time in your busy social life to take the bins out of the garage on a Monday evening and put them outside for the dustbin men to empty on a Tuesday morning? And every week.

They then need to go back into the garage when you come home on the Tuesday evening, do you see how this complex little system works? Out and then back in, out and then back in, not too hard to remember now is it? Out and then back in.

I know, you think that e-mail is very old-fashioned, that's why you haven't seen those funny things that I send you from time to time. But please take a look at them, they're sent with my love for you, and they will make you laugh. I know they will. They're fun. Some of them are just hilarious. You could try sending me some funny things from time to time too, eh?

Please. I love it when I make you laugh.

Re your lungs, don't smoke. Your generation knows so much more about the dangers associated with smoking, so why would you do it? Take a look at a photo on Google of a pair of lungs and then tell me that you want to poison yours with smoking. Disgusting habit, really, and they can and will never recover.

And no, you can't sleep in the same room as your seventeen year old girlfriend when she stays the night round here. I know you don't understand, but it's just how it is mate, all right? The spare room is a perfectly nice room for her to sleep in. Conversation ended.

Until next weekend of course, when you'll start asking me again.

About ten thirty in the evening, your dog likes to go outside for a walk. Yes, it's perfectly true that you could just open the door and let her out, but doggies don't always come back you see son. Not because they don't have a house key but for lots of reasons. "What's a dog?" Oh sorry, it's that lovely loyal chocolate brown Labrador in her basket down there that you said you would look after and take out for a walk every day, twice sometimes in one day you said, remember that conversation four years ago?

Yeah right.

Re security, when you take the emergency house keys out of the little safe box fixed onto the garage wall, do you think that you could then put them back in there when you have let yourself into the family house? That way you see they're there for the next person.

If you don't, then they may not be there for you next time, like last night at one in the morning when you came in late from a party. That was when you walked across the sopping wet grass again like you always do in the winter, with all of your hairy-faced mates!

Thank you so much, on behalf of the grass that used to be the colour green.

Re alcohol, yes you can have a beer from time to time, but don't just take one from the utility room, open it with a bottle opener, and then just appear at the table with the open bottle already in your hand. It's too late to throw it away then of course, as you know. It's part of your strategy isn't it? Just ask me first if you can have the beer with the meal, okay? But not every mealtime, okay? Or every day.

Oh, and sometimes it might be nice if you could contribute to the beer supply yourself from time to time. After all, you're the only one that ever drinks it!

We love you by the way, did we tell you that recently? Your turn.

Re our family home, we live in a very nice house. It has five bedrooms, two bathrooms, a double garage, our own driveway and a good garden. My first flat was so cold that it had ice on the inside of the windows. You expect to bypass this "flat stage" of life and go straight to the big family house don't you?

True?

We all love music in our family, don't we? I like to go into a music store and browse the selection of artists that they have there, walk out having bought some exciting new cds and then come home and unwrap them before placing them in my collection on a shelf, to play this new music perhaps later that same evening or weekend. For your generation, that's all far too old-fashioned and slow - you choose your tracks and download them in just a few seconds. No need to go out for music, park your car and go into the shop. Less packaging too, which is a good thing, right? My frustration comes from taking time to park the car, yours comes from the internet being slow to download today.

And keep the volume down to 20 maximum, would you? Please.

Parties are interesting things aren't they? For us your parents, ten or fifteen people coming round to the house one evening for drinks and those things that we call "nibbles", that's a party for our generation. It's fun, a bit different to the normal couples coming round for dinner, and who knows we might even still be up at 1 am?! For you lot, that's definitely not a party, it's only what you would all call a "gathering". What you call a party, for us that's "a rave". Parties, gatherings, raves, whatever.

Have fun! And be safe, all of you.

When I was your age, we would order an Indian take-away meal perhaps once or twice a month, it was only ever bought on a Saturday night and it was something special. You guys want it on a Thursday night, in the same week that you had a Domino's pizza on the Sunday evening, a Chinese meal on the Tuesday and a Subway 9 inch meal for lunch that same day.

Pace your ordering of take away meals, please.

You never read the newspaper! You're nineteen and I honestly don't think that I can ever remember seeing you sitting down with a drink to work your way through a daily paper. It can be fascinating, informative and helpful to you in your new life. Put the electronic screens down just once and read the paper, a real one, a paper one that leaves ink on your fingers afterwards.

It also leaves information in your head afterwards, and that's really good. Your head can take it you know.

Re domestic stuff, it's called "an iron" kids. Try it. Makes clothes look smart, and therefore you too. Turn it off after you've used it please, that way no one gets burned, like happened to your aunt last weekend.

If we live for something like eighty years, then at 52 I'm 65% of the way through my natural life. It could be a great deal more of course, we're not allowed to know, right? At 18 you're at about 22% of the way there. So that's why I seem to you so impatient, and why you seem to us to have no sense of urgency! Come on son, walk a little faster along the pavement, we haven't got all day you know!

I like my trousers to look good, what you might call "presentable". I like them to be comfortable, to fit well, to be well pressed, and ideally to match whatever other clothes I'm wearing that day. I might choose a work "look", or maybe a casual one, and they should ideally be easy to wash, clean and iron. A nice dark brown belt would look good with them too. Your generation chooses its trousers by label first, and the label simply has to be seen clearly, not necessarily with a huge label but with a label that is in the right place for those cool friends of yours who are "in the know" (you won't know this last phrase because you don't read books, remember?). You also wear a belt like me sometimes but one that seems to have a different purpose in life from my belt. You see, my belt was very definitely made to keep my trousers up whereas yours was made to keep them down, in place but down. Just how do you walk with them like that?!

I love you son.

Any chance you could put the toothpaste back onto the shelf after you've used it? Or empty the dishwasher for me? Wash the car that you get to drive maybe? Inside and out would be nice? Did you go and get its tyres inspected like I asked you to? Last month, remember?

Did you pay those cheques in for me like I asked you to? And did you get the dry cleaning for me on your day off? I hear Paulo called, he said he left a message with you when you answered the phone last Saturday morning.

Did you collect the new bag of dog food? Did you take her for a walk like I asked you to? The tumble dryer needs emptying, and could you put the nice clean sheets back onto your bed please? Ideally before you climb into bed later tonight.

The grass doesn't look any shorter, did you find time to cut it?

13. Landing on the White House Lawn

So, let's just think about it for a minute shall we? It's a very big topic after all, I mean really big in human terms, and it's well worth some study. Definitely, in my humble opinion.

Let's just make an assumption for a few moments that we humans are not the only life in the universe. (Take a big pause here please if you need it. it's fine really. And breathe deeply…)

Why on earth would we be? It seems an absurd proposition even to think that this might be the case. Do we really think that in the vastness of what we have come to call the local "back yard of space" that we can see looking out from this one planet, that we are really the only living beings to be found there? Surely not.

We have long uncovered an incredible fact, namely that there are more planets in the universe than there are individual grains of sand on this one planet that we live on! (Get your human mind round that one for a moment, you might want to sit down and run that by yourself again. More planets than there are grains of sand, - wow! Feel free to take another pause here if you need to, and to breathe deeply again too, that's all perfectly fine if you feel the need to do so.

It turns out that there are billions of them! Not tens of them, or hundreds, or thousands of them, or tens of thousands, or hundreds of thousands of them out there, not even a million or two million or twenty two million or thirty eight million or a hundred million, or one hundred and ninety nine million, but it turns out that there are many billions of other planets. Billions! Literally billions, of all sizes too. Try to think of the space that is needed to fit all of that in, it must be unimaginably huge compared to our tiny local and familiar world here on planet Earth. So given what we know, why then would this planet be the only one where there is life? It just doesn't make any logical sense. What would the point of all that other stuff be? It might be comforting for us to think that we're that important, but are we? Really? Does all of that vastness really centre around us as the only Life? I'm guessing … not. And you?

There are many people who take up the position that the universe actually has rather a lot of life going on in it. They hold the view that it's actually quite common and can be found in many parts, if only you can get there somehow. They subscribe to the theory that has become known as "Panspermia", which says that the conditions necessary for life are in fact all around us and therefore life can be found in many places. Large organisations like NASA and SETI (the Search for Extra Terrestrial Intelligence) are devoted to the exciting task of listening out for signs of intelligent life across the universe. They have massively expensive technology that is dedicated to this one single task, one hundred percent of the time, with sophisticated listening tools that are pointed towards different groups of planets where they have reason to think that there may be a planet at just the right distance from a local sun for life to have evolved there. Think Needle and Haystack here though.

This optimal position of planet to sun is known as "the Goldilocks Zone", and SETI's arrays of radio telescopes are out there night and day listening for any unusual kind of signal that can be heard.

The Goldilocks Zone is where you don't have the small bowl of porridge, or the big bowl, but you have the medium one which is just right. In other words the planet is not too hot or too cold but it is just right for Life, in terms of its distance from the Sun. Like Earth is from "our" sun.

In particular, they are looking for signals and patterns of sound that don't appear to be natural and ones that are not a regular part of the background noise of space, and which therefore may have been created artificially. A possible sign of Intelligent Life. Needle and Haystack though, remember?

So what have they found so far?

Nothing.

Or that's what we're told anyway, I wonder if they would actually tell us if they had really detected a signal, do you think they would? I reckon not, I have a friend who reckons that the military would be all over them immediately and take over their project in an instant. Just like they did in that film.

So, back to our initial assumption then, that there is other life in the universe. It seems to be a widely held view by those good people whose minds are open to this idea, that if the other bunch of space life was to come and find us that they would be far more advanced than we are. This is a simple conclusion based on the fact that they would have to possess far superior technology to ours (currently) in order to get across the vast distances in space and land safely on another planet. The exception here might of course be if they too originate from this same planet but we just don't realise it. If they too were based on Planet Earth, then it would make their journeys quite a lot easier. Let's assume for the time being though that they are extra-terrestrial and not intra-terrestrial.

However, we (that's Mainstream We) currently have no mainstream transport capability that could make such a journey across space. If you have studied what the Black Operations World may have then you may conclude that they do, of course. So it seems safe to assume that we would be talking here about a life form with far greater travel capability than we have. In other words, they have developed far better propulsion systems, the "holy grail" of space travel, than clever but crude chemical rockets. Ones that can warp Gravity around you so that you can travel at high speed and safely. And turn very cool right angles at high velocity too, that kind of thing! Which chemical rockets and conventional aircraft definitely can't.

Here is not the time or the place to explore the idea that we have in fact already developed such superior propulsion system ourselves, through reverse engineering of alien space craft that have either crashed or been deliberately brought down. There are far better people able to talk you through this argument than me. Many of them have written very exciting and well researched articles, essays and complete books on this subject. If you have yet to learn of this area, then go and feast yourselves on the books and other information available. It's an exciting subject to read about, but with frightening consequences too, given how some of the technology may have been acquired.

There is even suggestion that deals have been done, at the highest possible level, on an inter-species level that is. As far back as the 1950s in fact it has been suggested, and that those deals have even involved no less than an American President, personally.

There are several past Presidents of the US who are down on record at expressing their deep frustration at being unable to access stuff around the alien/ET topic. The President himself can't get to this stuff, really?! Just go back and watch Independence Day, it's all there for you to see. So this is big stuff, and these are truly amazing stories, but ones for another day, and for those better writers than me to tell you about.

Are you still with me? Pause as much as you need, and continue to take those big, deep breaths, as many as you like. It's a subject that has the ability to take a person's breath away for sure. For the moment let's content ourselves with the notion that other "intelligent" life exists, that it's definitely out there and that it has now reached the cosmic neighbourhood where we happen to live.

So then, when do they come knocking on our door? When would you? At what point do they make their impressive presence known to us? When would they decide that it's the "right" time to meet and talk? What could "right" possibly mean in this context, and "right" from whose point of view? Would this be when we have developed into animals that live in large and complex social groups and are clearly different from the wild animals that live around us? Would it perhaps be when we have found something that we call "Fire"? Or perhaps when we have made weapons that can kill successfully, or when we have developed powerful medicines that can heal, or what about the time when we invented that really useful thing called "the wheel"? Or things called Nuclear Bombs?

When exactly would be the "right" time? Maybe when our ability to reason was fully developed? Maybe when we understood our stewardship of this planet? Or perhaps when we had stopped killing and eating other animals just trying to live on this planet like we do? Perhaps we were visited hundreds of thousands of years ago by cosmic nomads, and instead of stopping over and meeting with us, they simply found that we were far too early in our development for their purposes and that we were just incapable of relating to them. Could be, timing matters you see. Maybe they just made some brief notes on their intergalactic iPads that we were best left alone for a few millennia before being re-visited, and then they just headed right back out into deep space at warp factor five. And that's fast, ask Captain James T Kirk of the Starship Enterprise!

Perhaps a time of something like a global war would be an appropriate time for the advanced guys to turn up and have an impact? Remember that in the second World War, there were some very interesting things seen in the skies above Europe called "Foo Fighters". These were like bright lights in the sky that often followed aircraft for quite some time, and we never did know what they were. The British pilots thought they came from the Germans, but they thought they were ours. Whose were they? Interesting...

The significant development of a nuclear capability is sometimes cited as something that alien races would watch here on Earth with interest and some concern too. When stories are told about large military planes carrying bombs or even aircraft carriers being tracked by large spacecraft, there seems to be the suggestion that we are being watched with regard to our ability to cause great devastation to the planet and to our own people around us. There are actually incredible stories of nuclear weapons being neutralized by other beings' technology either on the ground or in flight, and that they have the technology to literally turn off a missile as it sits parked in its silo/bunker or even as it is in full flight towards a target.

Do your research People. It's all so much easier these days, it's happened and there are complete books about it that we can all read. Of course you won't read such stories in your daily paper, nor hear it on the News at Ten. Hugh Edwards is never going to read that story out on the BBC News as you walk through the front door one evening after a hard day's work in the office. And rightly so, probably.

You may even doubt that such stories exist but exist they certainly do. Go and find out for yourself, it's good to be informed of the actual, and of the possible. And of what has been happening for many years.

The further suggestion is made that perhaps superior beings from other parts of space would have a clear perspective on our human existence that we can never have ourselves, and that perhaps they have seen this kind of deadly development underway before. Perhaps they too have had similar challenges in their own development as a race. Or in other races that they have been watching? Either way, the question must be asked when do the "guys up top" make themselves known to little us, all the way down here?

Maybe they know that they can never actually do this, at least not publically. Maybe they never will land on the White House Lawn, not because the grass has just been cut but because we humans couldn't deal with it as a very limited terrestrial species. A species of the summer green grass you might say, and not of the blackness of cold space. Maybe they already know with that special perspective of theirs that to do this openly really would lead to the immediate collapse of our society as we know it. Perhaps that's precisely why they keep their distance. Nice considerate chaps you see! Even we ourselves write in our books that if we found out that we were not the only species in the universe then our sense of place would shift in an instant. And forever. Whole religions would fail to cope with the arrival of other life forms. Belief systems would be turned upside down in a moment. The revelation that there are superior beings flying through our air space that we can do nothing about would likely induce panic. Who would retain any respect at that point for the military, or for the local police officer, or for that matter for a political man-made President? How would going into the office the morning after the landing on the White House lawn even be acceptable? We would have just witnessed one of the most significant events that can happen to the modest human race, and in an instant our lives would have been set in an entirely different context to the one that were living in just the day before. Put simply it would be Change, and change as big as Change can possibly be. Great day to be around though, don't you think? How much would you give to see that on Channel 4 News?

So, the question remains of when? When would they make their appearance? When would you? At what point would they feel justified, (if indeed they can feel things or even care about the concept of justice), in doing that? Some say that they would come to warn us against the development of our own lethal weapons. We've been giving out signals and data and radio programmes for many tens of years now.

Others put forward the idea that the "Weapon-ization" of space by mankind would be the moment when they rocked up. They would want to stop us building up arms up in space, it was bad enough on the ground. Why send them up into space, just how dumb are we?

Others suggest that our mishandling of the planet's delicate environment would be the spark for their very public arrival.

After all, even we know that this planet that we have the good fortune to live on is an absolutely exceptional one, it's just amazing, - ask Sir David Attenborough, he'll tell you.

Some say that's what the Crop Circle phenomenon is all about, we just don't get it yet. Yes, they are circles but more significantly they are messages. They just happen to be circular. In fact they're more varied than that. But whatever, if they did exist, at what point would they step in and be counted? The trouble is that as soon as you have developed something like the wheel, or the combustion engine, or television, or the power of flight, or a rocket that can break out of earth's gravity, you then go onto the next big thing and the previous stage seems less impressive and less likely to attract a vastly superior race. It's all relative again then. And of course relative to what the other guys are driving around in.

The next question, that you already have in your head of course, is why? Why would they step in? Why would you? If they have already done so, and many believe that they have, why have they done this? If they're so way ahead of us, what possible motive would they have in spending time (as we refer to it, I wonder what their word is?), with a race that is way, way behind them in so many ways? Just what possible reason could there be for them to do that? The possible answers that come to mind appear to range from good, through the not so good and onto to the worst scenario possible. "Good" appears to be that they have some kind of watching brief over us and that they care for us spiritually, that they are some kind of intergalactic guardian angels. Nice considerate chaps like I said earlier you see! The "not so good" says that they need resources badly from our planet that we also want to have access to, and that they have come here shopping for resources such as very specific minerals for example. The very worst idea is that we too are just another resource for them like water or gold or uranium could be. Think Laboratory rats here if you will, where the principle is turned back on us humans. We're the rats under that scenario. In other words, we are what they want, - this may not be good. Think how many people go missing around the world each year, particularly in the US. Hugh Edwards won't tell you about that on the news tonight either. He never would, because it wouldn't even reach him in the first place.

If that last one is true, it doesn't look good for us does it now?

The next question must be who would they make contact with? Governments? Heads of governments? The people who seem to build and control the weapons? So who then specifically?

The US? Britain? France? Mexico? Nato? Germany? Sweden maybe, or Norway? What about Russia? China? The United Nations in New York? David Beckham perhaps?

Some of them?

Three of them?

All of them?

None of them?

I don't know, I can only guess like you but it seems likely that governments and the military would get in on the act somehow doesn't it? Like they did in that film.

So, the next time that you have some time on your hands, go into the world of Google and look for some photographs of The Milky Way. Some of them are just breath taking to behold, particularly the ones where time-lapsed technology allows the light of the distant stars to come through into the image. The truly good ones let you know in a single instant how it got its milky name, there are just so many stars out there giving out light that it looks just like a sky of spilt white milk, The Milky Way. And it's out there all of the time, even though we don't see it during the daylight hours, or at night when it's cloudy down here.

And somewhere in there, amongst the millions of lights, there is Life, I promise you. Some of it has found us too. But for what purpose, we don't fully understand.

Then go outside and stare up at the real one stretching high above you in the night sky, and watch and think, and look and see, and question and reason, but be sure to see it all with your own eyes. Whenever you can.

It's Big Stuff, really big in human terms. And it's there all the time, watching back down at you as well.

Oh, one other final thing, you might need gloves some nights. And let us all hope they're keeping that White House lawn nice and tidy for the day when it gets landed on. I reckon they're doing precisely that.

14. What Role a Man?

"Oh yes hi, yes, I'll have a... um, I would like .... good morning ...I'll take a skinny latte please, yes, yes, thank you very much, yes perfect" said Keith, very politely. He had hesitated with his order just momentarily, as he was quite simply intimidated by her very considerable natural beauty. He hoped that she perhaps hadn't noticed his pathetic hesitancy but in truth how could she not have noticed? Even a nearby mouse would have.

For you see Keith was a polite man generally, in most situations and with most people. Modest, thoughtful and wracked daily by a deep insecurity, he made his way through his uncertain and now quite pointless life, as best he could. He coped, he existed, kind of. "Define that word "existed"?", - well let's say that at least he was still going. He was what you might call a survivor. He hadn't popped his clogs yet.

He liked his lattes, very milky, and these days they were one of his few real pleasures in life in fact. Only very occasionally he would take a bagel with some smoked salmon and cream cheese with his latte as well, but he did this a little less often nowadays than a few years back, since he was trying to reduce his body weight by the really precise figure of one and half stone. The exact timescales around this goal were really not that clear but the stated intention was there all right and the reduction in weight that was required was really very well known to him by now.

"That's about twenty one pounds in old money!" he would tell his friend. Deep inside he wanted to look better on the obvious outside, to feel better about his appearance, and particularly to look more attractive, which in turn would surely make him feel better. At least that's how his simple male thought process ran, if you could call that one idea a process. Keith and his mind eh, what was he like? But all of this mattered to him you see, now that he was in his "dangerous fifties".

"Say hi to Keith everyone!", a modest and well-meaning man in his fifties, who liked to find his little bit of personal space seated in warm cafes and the really predictable security that they brought him personally, at least until closing time anyway, which was generally around four thirty or five pm. He like being in coffee stores.

He took his coffee over to the table on a wooden tray, and the attractive young waitress told him that she would bring the creamy bagel over to him shortly. She was very attractive, as would the bagel be too that she would surely bring over to him in just a few minutes, thought Keith. The slightly heavy "fifty something" man sat down on the light beige wooden chair and placed the keys to his modest house and his new blue iPhone 5 down on the coffee table. He looked around smiling at the other people in the store. He looked around at them very slowly and casually, wanting to be in charge of his tray and his belongings and not to drop anything onto the floor, or do anything un-cool like that within her view, particularly dropping his brand new iPhone. She wouldn't be impressed by that now would she, Keith?

They were all seated in one of those very pleasant cafes that you find inside a Waterstones bookshop, slightly faded but comfortable enough, and that heady combination of fine words and the aroma of good coffee appealed to Keith rather a lot. The truth was that he was fast becoming addicted to it. The town outside was pretty mediocre to say the least, as were many of the local population leading their rather drab lives there too, but inside the cafe, inside the Waterstones branch in the very centre of the little town Keith felt safe, protected, and warm. Oh, and he felt a little inspired too. What inspired him of course were all of the wonderful books around him, for it was a powerful chance for Keith to be able to drink a well prepared hot coffee and to have his mind stimulated by good reading material physically within reach all around him. He also liked the structure of the solid wooden shelves and the very clear professional classification of all of the topics that could be studied therein. He liked the white laminated Category labels that had been used for they were the same kind of labels that he would have chosen were he the store Manager. He would often sit near the "Psychology" or the "Wellbeing" section, when the seats were available that is.

That sense of things being in order made him feel secure, it offered him a reference point you see, like he knew where he was in this oh so confusing world, at least for a brief while anyway. Would you believe that it almost gave him a sense of his place in the world, as he made his way through his drifter's life as best he could. At the moment, sitting where he had just taken his seat with his tray, he was somewhere between "Cookery" and "History", not too far from the "Health" section too which he could see slightly to his left. Wherever possible he preferred to find a table that was at least within direct sight of the "Self Help" section, he liked to do that whenever it worked out that way. This mattered considerably to Keith, providing him with an important reference point inside the bookshop, in much the same way as a dotted white line in the middle of the road does for the driver of a shiny new electric car. Some of the books there had come to be his greatest friends over many years, classics in their own right, legends in their own category, commercial blockbusters too some of them for their authors. You see he had found that you could always trust a good book, you could hold it in your hand, and you could smell its pages. Its words never changed from one day to another, it was impeccably consistent so you knew where you stood with a good book. Always.

Trust. And a good book.

He sipped his hot coffee and sure enough the delightful waitress was now coming over to him with his bagel. She had a great walk. She was more than just pretty, lots of girls are pretty, but she was rather beautiful, and Keith got her to linger at his table for just a few delicious moments, telling her how well she had made the food for him. She smiled a little, probably out of politeness more than anything else, and there was definitely a slight awkwardness to the moment, and all he could say to her was this:

"You're very good at what you do, thank you, you're very professional".

She definitely smiled again, the awkward moment had now happened again for the second time in just a few seconds, and she swished away briskly in her tight black pencil skirt to go back to the safety of her counter, hiding a little from him behind the salad and condiments bar. Keith felt clumsy, oh so very clumsy, and he wished that better words had come to his head and tumbled out of his mouth. Some younger words would have been good too, but tragically they had eluded him when they were most needed. He would have to work on that next time, to do some clever preparation around some cool new words, if indeed there was a next time. She was quite, quite beautiful to him.

How he would love to have the good fortune of spending several hours with her across the dinner table. Nothing formal, something pretty casual would be just fine, a young and really informal environment would do actually, no frilly pink tablecloths and napkins, nothing cheesy like that, no hovering waiter, no Blue Nun wine or prawn cocktail. More a modern casual noodle bar, yes that was the kind of thing he had in mind. Not that his remarkably attractive waitress friend in her tight black pencil skirt had any idea of his thoughts of course.

He ate into the bagel slowly, his warm tongue enjoying its smooth and moist texture, it was every bit as good as it looked, and very creamy too. She had done a great job, and he stirred his milky coffee a few times very deliberately with the fashionable silver spoon, making an opportunity not once but twice to casually glance over in her direction as he moved his long spoon slowly in and out through the bubbly smooth froth. She was wearing a black top that fitted her quite tightly, tight but not too tight as she needed to do lots of bending down at the counter. She bent well. She was a good bender, if such a term exists. And he glimpsed that she had a name badge on too, in a dark green colour, but he couldn't quite read it from where he was sat. He would make a point of taking in her name from the badge on her chest when he went over to pay the bill. He fancied that she might be Italian, or Turkish maybe, something like that because of her long dark hair and exotic dark skin colour. About twenty five too he guessed. She possessed a very powerful natural grace for Keith. What long fingers she had as well. There, she was bending down again to reach the cream cheese. Wow, she was really good at bending.

She did catch his eye at one point after this as she stood up with a silver dish nearly overflowing with oily tuna, fresh cucumber and mixed peppers and his new Goddess friend smiled at him for just a very brief moment, before spinning round to grasp a heavily seeded ten inch granary roll from the baker's wicker basket behind her, taking it firmly in her right hand. Yes, she had definitely seen him looking at her, with his big sturdy spoon in his hand, but then again perhaps she was just being polite. This was very possible. He took some more bites from her warm bagel, it tasted so good, and he washed it all down with some more of the frothy latte.

He had originally planned to look through the "Self Help" section that morning for some new stimulating reading, to make some new "friends". He already had all the classic self-help books you see, and that means all of them really, but what he wanted now was some material that would actually provide him with some of the answers to his very personal experience of life, answers that he so desperately craved. The first wave of reading on this subject had piqued his interest but it had had not really delivered great insight of any kind. He was very disappointed it had to be said, and he was still thirsty for answers. Perhaps the world of self-help was just an industry like any other that made money in this case for the author and publisher alike, and which really delivered nothing more in a book than some fairly obvious thoughts, a few predictable ideas and some really very modest concepts only. Perhaps the reader of this genre of literature was so completely open to anything that fitted in even vaguely with their own conclusions about life that anything similar and sensible in these kind of books would be taken as pure genius. Good news for the author and publisher alike then!

The Turkish Goddess was now putting the heavy dish of tuna, cucumber and mixed peppers back now, holding her pose just long enough to position temptingly the silver dish in order to show the oily offering at its best deep inside the glass cabinet to her next hungry Customer.

He finished his coffee. It had been very enjoyable. He gathered his things up now, stacked the side plates and cutlery onto the tan-coloured melamine tray very considerately just for her, placing them all towards the centre of her tray to make it safe for her to carry it away, and then stood up very slowly. A very mild running injury from the previous evening's run was feeling slightly uncomfortable this morning and so he rose to his feet slowly, smiling at those around him again. She just might find him quite cool if he did it this way, even if only for a moment, for that would be enough. His new phone was placed deliberately into the black rucksack, the keys to his modest property too, some loose change was gathered in too, and then a single heavy and gold pound coin was subtly slid across the table to rest beside the olive oil bottle in the middle of the little round table. That was for his Turkish Goddess, a little gesture that was all, not that she will ever need money he thought with inherent beauty like that. If only she knew the power given to her by her natural beauty, her female power, but then again perhaps it was better that she did not become aware of this, not yet at least, for that would surely spoil her attractive innocence. Turkish Delight indeed …

He changed his mind and he delivered the tray to her on the counter, momentary eye contact being made between server and customer, and more stupid, dumb, middle-aged words fell out of his stupid, dumb, middle-aged mouth again. Not even one of them was cool. She took the tray and turned to place it on the counter behind her, near the kitchen entrance.

"So how much do I owe you then, Marta?" he asked, cleverly taking in her first name from her badge proudly positioned on her chest and building that very personal detail into his question to her in just an instant. Keith was sharp, by surname and by personality too you see. She looked good in her tight black outfit.

"This will be four pounds, please", she said in a distinctly Mediterranean accent.

"I'm really sorry, but I only have a twenty pound note.... it's a crisp fresh one, I've just printed it you see!"

More crap and clumsy middle-aged words Keith, not so sharp are you now?

She processed his crisp fresh note, giving him the correct change of sixteen pounds, and handing him a small receipt from the till too, for she was indeed very professional as he had correctly observed to her earlier. She said thank you, but she didn't even look him in the eye this time, and turned away to go over to the microwave behind her that was bleeping away telling her that the bowl of tomato and basil soup was now ready to be served to a waiting Customer at one of the tables. Keith stayed where he was for just a few seconds more, and she must have sensed this in some way, because she stopped and turned back round to look directly at him.

"Was there something else you wanted, Sir?" she asked him looking into his hungry face.

"Yes please?"

Keith paused.

"No, that's all fine, thank you. You're very good at what you do, you're very professional", replied the invisible man, and she continued on her way, and then went out into the table area to serve the bowl of heated-up soup to her waiting Client.

In her black pencil skirt.

Keith left the cafe area. He headed for the psychology book section. He wanted to find a good basic guide on Communications, something like that, or on Body Language. His Goddess friend did not watch him atall to see where he was going to. Besides, she was busy and she had other Customers to attend to. Nor would she even remember him a few minutes later, for the café had many invisible men that chose to come in and buy a cup of good coffee from her. The truth was that they came and they went and many of them would kindly leave her a one pound tip too, like Keith had.

He worked his way through the "Psychology" section, looking for something around Communication skills, Body Language would be helpful too, when his attention was caught by a red paperback book called "Have you found your purpose?"

"No I haven't" he said to himself ever so quietly. He picked it up, and began to read the author's introduction. It was written especially for men, and there on the very first page was a very appropriate question:

"Have you ever felt that you lack purpose, and that somehow you are invisible to others around you?"

Keith bought the book.

15. A very Personal Lockdown

It was getting serious now. Not that serious here in the UK though compared to some other countries in Europe but it was plenty serious enough.

Italy was suffering terribly. And they didn't really seem to know why. She was losing many hundreds of people a day. Some days it was getting close to a thousand deaths, not over a week but in a single day. Some said it was because they had a population with a higher proportion of elderly people and many of them had caught the virus early on before the spread was even known or the virus was identified. Others conjectured that several key individuals had travelled back there from visits to China and had been spreading the virus locally but unknowingly for several weeks, and by then it was too late to halt the spread of infection. This was a virus that travelled well. Sometimes in a First or a Business Class cabin too.

Whatever the truth, the spread of the virus in the Northern part of Italy around Lombardy was proving to be the worst in the whole world. On the graphs that would be shown over the forthcoming weeks, Italy was at the top but for the wrong reasons. These were graphs where you wanted to be nowhere near the top, not like you did in your class chart at school. For these were graphs where the nearer to the bottom of the chart that you were, the better, alongside countries like Germany and South Korea. They both appeared to be doing something that few other countries were and that's where you wanted your country to be, near the low death figures, and not up at the top.

Spain too. She was suffering very nearly as badly. Her daily fatality figure was regularly around eight hundred for far too long now. Similar theories went round about the older people in the population there, as in Italy, and that just like Italy so Spain had a society that revolved around the family very much and so there would be many gatherings of families in close proximity to each other. Naturally, the virus could spread easily in this way, and it did. There were heart breaking stories too of relatives being unable to get into Care Homes across Spain to see if their elderly loved ones were even still alive in there. Sometimes they were, sadly sometimes they weren't. What must the pain level of Grief have been like in both countries during these weeks? Our hearts went out to them. Perhaps travelling there on holidays would never be the same again.

There was a word that they all started to use about now. It was a word that our ears soon got used to hearing. Everyone came to use it. Journalists, Politicians, Commentators, Health professionals, Economists, Head Teachers, News readers interviewing people, sports players, Police Officers, Ambulance Drivers…. they all confirmed that we were going through "unprecedented times". It's an adjective that comes from the Latin verb "praecadere" meaning to fall or happen before – yes, these were times when nothing like this had happened before. "Unprecedented" times indeed. At least not in living memory. We had experienced Sars, and something similar called Mers, and there were always outbreaks of Flu in the Winter time, certainly here in the UK. Sometimes they would claim up to twenty five thousand deaths over the Winter period, at least somewhere around that figure was thought to be contributed to do by the "humble" flu. Not so humble then.

But this was more, much more. Like nothing that we had known in our lifetimes. Therefore, by logical definition, we all found ourselves living in "unprecedented" times. Sadly, some were dying in them too, and hundreds of our nation by the day.

This was an epidemic. We soon came to see that. But more than that it was an epidemic that had spread to a large area. And that was how we define a pandemic, a disease that has now spread to a large area, and this one was definitely under no control whatsoever. It was out of control, and raging like a bushfire. But globally, for unlike a fire it travelled successfully over water too. And so on the 11th of March 2020, the World Health Organisation labelled it as a "Pandemic" officially. Equally concerning were the comments by Dr Tedros Adhanom Ghebreyesus, the chief of WHO, who said at that point that he was:

"deeply concerned … by alarming levels of interaction".

He meant on the part of National Governments and Administrations. He would encourage them all to "Test, Test, Test" immediately. Some were quicker to respond to his professional guidance than others, as Time would show. The UK did not do well in this area, not at all. Valuable time was lost.

That same day, one country took some action. Hours later, shops would close in Italy. Only food shops and pharmacies would be allowed to be open. The country's Prime Minister, Giuseppe Conte, explained to his nation that if your café, restaurant, hairdressers or bar could not guarantee at least one metre of distance between you and your Customers, then they should all close. Immediately. So too should all non-essential company departments. This they did.

And so we would become familiar with the concept of "Social Distancing". It turns out that this concept would be around for a long time. As would the buying of bottles of antiseptic hand gel, that particular activity for a very long time to come in fact. That was a good market to be in too by the way as many chemists ran out of supplies more or less overnight. We reached a point where humble bottles of hand gel were being rationed out to queuing Customers. Perhaps such things as Distancing and having gel to hand had by now even inserted themselves into the Nation's Psyche. Like the term "9/11" had too. Even young kids soon spoke about "Social Distancing". Perhaps that term was harder for the older folks to understand, and to stick to though.

In the UK, the situation was developing, and like the spread of the virus, it was developing fast. It seemed to have come out of the blue somehow, from a place over in China. That place was called Wuhan but that was their problem, wasn't it somehow? For they were over five thousand miles away and it could only be their problem, right? It couldn't get over here, not in significant numbers surely? It was an Asian thing, right? It was on their continent, and not ours, right? It would stay there basically, and blow over in time, surely? These things fade away and die over time, don't they? Yes, like Sars did, right? See? That came and went, like these things do, from time to time. And it won't be allowed to cross into other countries, we were sure of that. Besides, we have a flu epidemic every Winter and so it's like a version of that, right? Don't worry, you'll be fine. It's a natural and a cyclical thing. Just like it came, so it would go. Such were the thoughts going through the Nation's Head.

Wrong. This thing spread quickly. That was one thing that became very clear. Over time anyway. The Head of The WHO would go on to say that with this particular virus, the way up was extremely quick, and the way down much slower. In others words this became a very real issue very quickly, that would take a much longer time to go away. If it did that at all. It went from something five thousand miles away to a Threat to your own family here in the UK in a matter of a few weeks. It appeared to have come out of nowhere but we needed to get past that idea rapidly. Life depended on how we now responded.

A particular aspect of the COVID-19 Pandemic was the timing. It arrived as we were coming out of the Winter and heading into Spring. This can be a wonderful time of year when the daffodils, the blue bells and the snowdrops come out and we begin to look forward to warmer and brighter days. A time of year when in one special weekend the clocks are put forward by one hour and suddenly we get our evenings back! Somehow the fact that it is then light until about seven thirty into the evenings makes us think that the Winter is behind us and we start to look forward to the Summer. A time of year of course when many people start to book their Summer Holidays too. But not this year, not in 2020. This year, this was just one thing that would be different. One of so very many things. You could dream of them but don't even think about booking holidays. BA grounded seventy per cent of their fleet, and their shiny planes were seen parked up by the side of the runway at Heathrow, like Ford Mondeos at an NCP. Virgin Atlantic were struggling badly, but apparently not enough for Richard Branson to dip into his pocket. That would be the pocket with an estimated $5.1 billion. It's actually quite a large figure, in any currency that you might choose.

So, British Spring time arrived officially at one am on Sunday 29th of March this year, like it had done last year around this time, and the year before that, and the year before that. But this year would be different, and memorable too, and for many a very frightening year too. And quite quickly too. It was all like we were living in some sort of dream and many felt that we would surely just wake up soon and find that it had been exactly that. It had a strong sense to it of just not being real. Like something out of a Netflix boxset, the real "Epidemic" or "Contagion". And I think that the arrival of Spring, a time of warmth and growth and promise, a time of New Birth, but which quite simply was bringing Death with it this time made it all very unreal. People spoke of a bad dream, about how unreal it all seemed, and there were discussions of whether or not we were actually living in a "Parallel Universe". Had this happened as we were going into the dark and cold of Winter it might possibly have been even harder for the Nation. But this was going to be bad enough. As we would see.

Not easy being a Leader is it? At the best of times, it's not an easy thing to get right. Much is expected of you by those around you. Particularly when you're new to being a Supervisor or Team Leader, a Manager or a Director…. or a Prime Minister too. Boris had a big enough workload as it was. It had just got harder and with decisions to take that carried far greater implication. Being a Prime Minister definitely just got to be a matter of Life and Death, if it wasn't that already. We started to see him on the television giving us updates on the Government's response and their plan to defeat the epidemic. Amongst the many things that were in his Job Description were now a series of decisions that he would need to take about the very safety of the Nation. Men, Women and Children.

At times of crisis, many discussions are had and many experts suddenly come to the fore. And many discussions were had about what the Prime Minister's next step would be, as the disease spread throughout the UK. People began to say that he had little room to manoeuvre, if any. In these unprecedented times there were some precedents set by other countries though, like Italy for example with their Lockdown, and amongst the informed people who watched the News and read the Papers and who tuned into Current Affairs programmes, one thing became pretty well inevitable – Lockdown. Meaning that the British Prime Minister would soon have to make a Key Decision with regard to the safety of the Nation, and potentially do what other countries had done. The Virus brought its own vocabulary along with it, with words such as Pandemic, WHO, Social Distancing, Challenges, Pivoting, Nightingale Hospital, PPE and now Lockdown.

On the evening of Monday March 23rd, we were presented with his decision. The Government was telling us, not advising us, to work from home, wherever possible. For at least three weeks. There was to be no non-essential travel, such as going into your regular offices, and no Public Gatherings of any kind. Including Football fixtures. Schools, Colleges and Universities were all to close immediately. Some businesses would remain open by definition of what they provided – Supermarkets, Food Shops, Pharmacies, Health Shops, Parks too, hardware stores, petrol stations, bicycle shops, pet shops, corner shops, laundrettes, car rental offices, newsagents, post offices, banks, and to many people's relief, Off licences too were all permitted to continue in business. Supply of your favourite beer would not be interrupted, for the time being then!

Those businesses that were ordered by the UK Government to shut included cafes, pubs, workplace canteens, bars and nightclubs, hair & beauty salons, auction houses, car showrooms, libraries, playgrounds, gyms, community centres, cinemas, places of worship, galleries & museums, swimming pools and leisure centres, casinos, spas and skating rinks. Alas the beauty of the Nation, our hairstyles, the borrowing of library books, the speed dating scene, buying a new little black dress, meeting a mate for a cheeky beer, bumping into someone over a coffee in Costa, and chatting with someone on the treadmill next you at the gym, all these things would have to go on hold. Sorry People. Even the imminent purchase of your gorgeous Aston Martin in British Racing Green would need to go on hold too. It would have to wait, we had another priority, as a Nation.

Perhaps the Birth Rate into 2021 might go up, but then again there were lots of very practical reasons why it might do the very opposite of course. And there might be many more separations and divorces as a result of a sustained period of National Lockdown over time. Sadly, it was noted too on the sidelines that there would inevitably be a rise in things like Domestic Abuse, and Domestic Violence. Inevitably, for the conditions were perhaps now in place more than ever before.

Who'd be a Prime Minister in the unprecedented times of a Pandemic? Well, Boris Johnson was, and he had to deal with whatever scenarios were presented to him. It wasn't what he ever thought that he would be dealing with in Politics probably. Brexit yes, issues in Education and International Trade for sure, Financial Topics yes, regular Health challenges too definitely, Climate Issues, and maybe even going into a war, but not this particular war. For the Human Population was now fighting against a deadly and invisible enemy that went under the name of COVID-19. Enemy Missile Bases would be so much easier to target.

And so public expectation came to be met. We found that what we had expected by way of the Prime Minister's decision was indeed now in place, and immediately. We were in a state of Lockdown. Officially and legally, and most definitely morally. "Stay at Home, Protect the NHS, Save Lives." Perhaps this three-part message entered into the Nation's psyche about now too. A bit like the railway's three-part message of "See it, Say It, Sorted" but a thousand times more significant. If only we could just see it, just say it, and just get it sorted.

Analogies were drawn about this time to how the situation was just like going for a run, and it was made clear to us that we now found ourselves "Not in a sprint but in a Marathon". This was a long-term thing then, with timescales unknown by any human alive. And it would turn out that the Time of Lockdown became very different to each and every one of us involved. The people of the UK were to have a very personal Lockdown, depending on their Life Circumstances.

Sarah was fine with it. Well, she would be wouldn't she? She was just ten years old. She had just been told by her Mum and Dad that she wouldn't have to go to school for the rest of the term. And possibly into next term too – Yippee! So no lessons then, and no rotten old homework? And no double maths lessons then with Miss Herbertson on a Friday morning? I don't even have to wear a uniform, I can wear my favourite clothes? Awesome! But then too the realisation that she couldn't get to see her friends for quite a while. And she couldn't pass her exams in Spanish and English that mattered so much to her, or take part in the swimming competition that she trained for so well after school and at the weekends. And she wouldn't get to see her class mates for many months? Or meet her friend who was leaving at the end of the school year as she was moving away from the area. Also, she had left her bag at school with her favourite cardigan and trainers in it, in her locker she thought, and would she be able to go and get that this week for the sleepover party next weekend? Which of course would now not be going ahead. Such was Sarah's lockdown.

Her Dad Kevin worked in the IT industry. He worked in Sales, Corporate Sales. So this was going to be an interesting time then? No ability to go out and see his Customers face to face, and certainly no more hand shaking for the foreseeable future. He was a Sales Manager too and so now he would need to lead better than ever before with his team of seven Corporate Account Managers. He would need to inspire them at a point in time when he himself was lacking in Inspiration. He would have to call on his boss Peter but he was about as useless as a chocolate teapot. There were Sales Directors and then there was Peter. Also, he didn't have an office at home, they only had a small house and his wife Becky had already converted the back bedroom into her home office. He would have to get a box of some kind and work out of that down on the kitchen table in some way. Still, he wouldn't have the three hours of commuting each day, so that was a good thing. Both for him, and for the planet. The other thing was that he and Becky had not been getting on well recently, not at all well in fact. That was going to make this a very difficult time for the family, and no doubt he wouldn't get any relief on his Sales Targets either, so the financial pressure wouldn't go away. This was not going to be easy then, and he wasn't sure how well he would cope. And Peter was not going to add any value, that was for sure! He gulped at the thought, and went out to the garage to look for a large cardboard box to keep his stuff in. He'd have to buy a new stapler too of course. Flipchart too, and those weren't cheap.

Dave drove a Number 11 Bus, in the centre of London. He'd been doing that route for a few years now. Things had changed in the thirty years that he'd been in the job, and the latest Routemaster bus was actually a pretty good vehicle to drive. It was powerful and automatic, and it came with good air conditioning for the summer. Not a bad place to be overall then on a Tuesday afternoon, that's if you have to go to work, and even the driver's seat was comfortable. Much improved over the older bus he drove before on the number 9 route.

He had another eighteen months to go before he retired, and he was so looking forward to that time, when he could get up even earlier in the morning to go and play his beloved golf. He was never going to be the World's best golfer but for him, that was not what it was all about. It was about relaxing, doing something that he enjoyed, meeting a few mates to play a full round of eighteen holes with, and then having a cheeky pint with them on "the 19th hole". Heaven for him, and he couldn't wait. He'd keep out of Sheila's hair during the day too, and they could get together over dinner when she closed her hair salon about 5.30 pm. With a nice glass of that Pinot Grigio wine from Sainsburys too, yes, that would all be very nice, that was all going to be lovely to look forward to. He would swing by the doctor's though on the way home and book an appointment with Doctor Ashton. He wasn't feeling that great today, he had a dry cough that had come on in the past twenty four hours, and he had a few aches and pains too, so he thought that he's get it all checked out.

A week later, his bus on the number 11 route was being driven by someone else. The golf and the cheeky beers on the 19th hole might have to wait ….

Babs loved dogs. And dogs loved Babs. Five years ago she quit her job as a secretary in an engineering company, and as she used to say to her girlfriends across in the local pub … "I engineered a different career for myself!" How they laughed over coffee at that one! She now had her own private company called "Paws for Thought", a dog walking company. Which she used to explain to her girlfriends was very different to "a Dogging Company"! How they laughed at that one too. And at the size of the balls on the German shepherd too out walking one morning. Her friend Kasha said that she used to go out with a German, he wasn't a shepherd but come to think of it, he had big balls as well! How the girls laughed at that one too. One of them even spilt her coffee over her new Primarni blouse, she had found that so funny! The Truth was that Bab's business was very up and down during the lockdown. Some of her regular clients had stayed with her, but the other half explained that since they would be working from home now, that they might as well be taking their own dogs out for a walk themselves. Or "Wanking from Home" as Kasha liked to call it. And yes, they all laughed at that one too! So her income nearly halved but then again a few new people had called her after the card she placed in the local Coffee shop, up on their green notice board, had brought in some new enquiries. So overall, her head was above water and besides she was doing what she loved, being out walking lovely doggies of all shapes and sizes, and particularly not being stuck in a boring office surrounded by clever but dull engineers in grey rubber shoes and with pens in the breast pocket! That's why she did what she did, after all. And yes, Kasha was right, that dog did have simply enormous balls. Bigger than engineers' they all agreed, and how they laughed at that idea too!

Klaudia ran a coffee shop. It was rather nice, and it was very individual. She was very happy in her work. And she had recently taken on two new staff members. Part time yes, but she planned to move them up to full time around Easter time, if they needed the work. Yes, life in "The Coffee Store" was pretty okay. She had many regulars, a lot of other people who would drop in on their way to somewhere, and then local people who could come in mid-morning too. She would never make a fortune from this place but like Babs, she did what she did because she enjoyed it. She had recently entered into a contract with a local company that supplied cakes and pastries to her, and they did some wonderful gluten-free products too. They weren't cheap mind but people had now started to ask for them specifically as soon as they came in and they seemed to sell very well. Like "hot cakes" you might almost say!

Her business began to suffer when they were only allowed to serve take-away food. That actually held up surprisingly well but they were running at about seventy percent of their former weekly turnover maximum. She hoped very much that this would soon be over and some kind of Normality would return. She kept the place spotlessly clean in preparation for that wonderful day, with all of the tables and chairs wrapped in an industrial polythene. The flowers were still fresh every day though. Even in the weeks before this point though, she had noticed that people had seemed hesitant about coming into a public place, like a café, and sitting down in close proximity to lots of other people. The young Mums with toddlers had mostly stopped coming in, and the local elderly folks had stopped coming in all together. Except that is for Old Tom, who was in his nineties. He said that the Germans hadn't got him, nor had the Winter Flu, so he was dammed if he was going to stay stuck indoors all because of some yellow flu from China – besides, he never ate Chinese food! Bless him. He always had the same, a pot of English Breakfast Tea and two slices of Brown toast, and dark orange marmalade. Bread to be cooked on one side only though. And he always had the right money every time. One of Life's regulars was Tom. But yes, generally it was getting tough, and then when the Government order came to shut shop, or shut café, that was devastating. Klaudia had no other source of income you see. She wouldn't be buying those nice gluten-free products from her friend for quite a while now, but even then there had been some disagreement over what it said in the contract that she had signed. The painful bit was how rapidly it had all happened. It had been really quick. She had to let got her part time workers immediately and look for another job herself. She felt lucky to get a position as Café Manager in the local Tesco, part time, but as they say "Every Little Helps".

Jane was a nurse. Jane was a very good nurse, her colleagues would describe her as "dedicated", simple as that. And Jane worked in Intensive Care. Have a guess what her Lockdown was like. Probably about as bad as it gets. Very different to running a dog walking business or running a pleasant coffee shop. She went to work just like so many of us, and simply risked her life every day that she did. Just by going into her place of work, in her case an NHS hospital. Fortunately for her, her hospital managed to get a good supply of Personal Protection equipment. Although she had one or two difficult days, she had coped about as well as was possible in the circumstances. The PPE kit was hot and it was uncomfortable and since she wore glasses it was even more uncomfortable to work in. Early on, there had been several shifts when they weren't sure if they would have the kit, the necessary kit, for the next shift. So they had taken it off, washed it down with antiseptic wash designed for similar tasks, and then placed it carefully in a dedicated store room in the event that they would need it again the next day. Or perhaps one of their colleagues might. Either way, it was there if it was needed. They say that a nice cup of coffee is a "life saver" after a hard morning's work, well these piece of personal protection kit were literally life savers, potentially. For these were heroes going into Intensive Care day in day out, shift in, shift out and performing minor miracles every day. Ask their patient in St. Thomas Hospital in London, called Boris Johnson, if they performed miracles. They rarely took their breaks, it was hot and uncomfortable work, and clearly it was sometimes highly dangerous work. Sometimes they wouldn't even remember to drink water or have more than a biscuit or a cheap sandwich during an entire shift. And very often their dedication carried them into extra hours beyond the official hours of their shift. And remember, many of these medical professionals had their own loved ones back at home waiting to see them return home safely. One of the cruellest aspects of this virus too was that the loved ones of the patients who were in serious trouble were not allowed into the Intensive Care Unit to see them or to look into their eyes or to hold their hands, before they slipped away. So professional Intensive Care Nurses like Jane and her colleagues not only looked after their patients in the clinical sense but they also held their hands and played the role of the last person that they would ever see, talk to or perhaps even laugh with before they joined the daily statistics of COVID 19 deaths. Who trained them for that? Jane said she didn't remember being trained for these things. And after her shift, she would go home, only to come back in to the same "stuff" on her next shift. It never got any better. There were two things she found particularly tough. The first was if the patient was a young person, some of whom had no other known physical health issues. They were apparently perfectly healthy people otherwise. The second was when they had to nurse one of their own colleagues on the ward, turned from Nursing Staff member to Patient themselves. Sometimes this change happened in less than twenty four hours, it could be that fast. And for Jane and her dedicated colleagues it was like this for week after week after week …. That was how the Lockdown was for her.

Bill walked out onto the stage looking quite smart. He didn't stride out boldly but then it wasn't a slow kind of entrance either. You might say that it was confident and shall we say purposeful. This is Bill Gates by the way. You know Bill right, yes that Bill! The richest man in the world kind of Bill. He had some smart grey trousers on, we might still call them slacks perhaps, and a cool pink V Neck jumper. I think he had a white shirt underneath, and he was wearing some dark tan slip on shoes. No doubt the whole outfit cost thousands of dollars but he looked cool and comfortable. Even the richest man cares how he looks I guess. He was here today to talk about something that was hugely important and his sense of purpose showed through, despite his calm and slightly jovial manner, to begin with. He was giving a TED talk about the epidemic and how the virus spreads. He spent some time giving the background to it and put it into context with regard to other diseases that we had experienced in recent years. He spoke about Sars, Mers and Ebola too. He was clearly knowledgeable and he also shared some good detail on what the Bill and Melinda Gates Foundation was doing to help in this important field. Bill Gates didn't talk for too long this time, perhaps about twenty five minutes all together, something like that in total. You can find it easily on YouTube yourself, that's if you're interested. He was fluent, he knew his stuff and he was clearly passionate about it. Oh, one other thing, this TED talk that he gave, the one where he is wearing the pink V Neck jumper and dark tan shoes… that was back in 2015. Some four to five years ago the authorities were more than aware of the possibility of such an Epidemic happening, probably a Pandemic in fact, and there were many discussions that were had at that time about how they could be prepared for it. Here was Bill Gates then warning us about something exactly like COVID 19 coming along nearly five years ago, sometime back in 2015. Meetings did take place we were informed, committees were formed too and discussions no doubt took place between Pharmaceutical/Research Organisations and National Governments. We may never know all of the details of discussions around that time but Bill Gates' TED talk, the one where he is wearing his pink V Neck jumper, makes it clear that the progress that was needed then was not made. For whatever reason. No wonder then that Bill was interviewed regularly for his thoughts and views when the real Pandemic actually happened in early 2020. This was a man who would surely continue to have much to contribute to this important and most urgent debate on what was now a very real Global Health Crisis. Not an imaginary one. You know, the one that Bill Gates had been warning us about nearly five years ago, wearing his smart pink V Neck jumper and grey slacks. The world should have listened to him better then.

The journalists were kept busy during the whole Pandemic, as you might imagine. Writing, blogging, doing face to face interviews and then when Social Distancing came in doing so remotely in Conference Calls. And some worked better than others, there were not unsurprisingly a few technical issues along the way, here and there, but most of the Conference calls went well enough. Some of the higher profile journalists were invited along to the Cabinet Office Briefings at No.10 Downing Street, and initially these were led by Boris Johnson, the British Prime Minister. He bounced out like Tigger from the Green Room behind, (perhaps since renamed The Blue Room?), normally with two Medical Advisors either side of him. And the format would soon become very familiar to us, as the PM led the Daily Briefing, sharing whatever information he chose to give out, before handing over to the Medical Experts to say their piece and bring us up to date on their areas of expertise. Standing to the right of the PM, was a very tall man, Professor Chris Whitty. He is Chief Medical Officer (CMO) for England, the UK government's Chief Medical Adviser and head of the public health profession. He is a tall and very thin man, who always wore a dark grey suit and white shirt and normally with a red tie, to begin with. His tie colour would move over time to darker blue for many of the Cabinet Room Briefings. He gave us confidence I think. There was something of The Headmaster about him. He gave the very clear impression that he knew his stuff and he was not to be messed with. If a Journalist ever tried to put words into his mouth or if they quoted something inaccurately, he would firmly and immediately correct them and put the record straight. If you remember the way the HeadMaster made you feel at school, then you have it. Whether he was a naturally assertive man or he had been through some Media Training, either way he appeared strong and confident. And I think the Nation very soon came to trust him. Being tall in stature certainly did him no harm. To the left of the Prime Minister stood Sir Patrick Vallance, the Chief Scientific Advisor to the Government. His role is to advise Government on all Scientific and Technology Issues, and he cut a rather different character in the Briefings than did Professor Whitty. Sir Patrick favoured a button down collar shirt, perhaps a little more casual in its style, and somehow he came over as more academic than the CMO did. Did we trust him as much as we did Chris Witty, I would suggest not. He would do well to take a leaf out of Professor Whitty's book and keep his hands still when talking. Letting your words speak for themselves is so much more powerful than allowing your hands waving around do your talking for you, particularly when the subject is a grave one like Life and Death. But we were sure that he was competent enough, and he was a key participant in the Government's Daily Briefings from No. 10 Downing Street.

Sometimes, other Cabinet members would lead the Daily Briefings in place of the Prime Minister. When he fell ill of course this was the only way. Some did better than others, one or two failing and failing utterly to show the required empathy that the National Crisis demanded so very clearly. The Health Secretary was having a very tough time many thought, as he tried hard to deliver the message that the Government of Boris Johnson was doing everything that it could to get Personal Protection Equipment out to NHS hospitals up and down the country. Doubtless Matt Hancock was and is a very decent man. However, there was a continual disconnect between the message that he was giving out in these Briefings and the stories that were coming back in from the NHS staff themselves, up and down the country, about what was actually reaching them. And of course the reality of that situation was that too many of them would pay the ultimate price for treating infected patients without the necessary medical protection. Day after day we heard tragic stories of committed NHS Workers losing their lives, for doing nothing more than going into their place of work.

The role of the investigative journalists remained as it always had. By now, Boris Johnson had explained in one of the early Briefings that the Government would wish to apply its own Social Distancing measures and that the Cabinet Briefings would very soon require no Journalists to be physically present in the Cabinet Briefing, as they moved over to remote sessions. Their role to hold the Government to account publically would still go on but through the medium of Conference Calls and Remote technology instead, and generally these sessions ran smoothly. The PM had promised that the Journalists would still have equal access to the Participants in the Daily Briefings and would be able to ask them the same questions as they would were they in the room just a few feet away from him. For this was a Crisis the like of which we had never known and one that would keep the Journalists all round the world very busy for a very long time. Stories did not come any bigger than this. Not just the UK but the entire Human Population was in a global Pandemic. This had not happened since The Spanish Flu of 1918/19, in which something like five hundred million people had been infected by the virus. Up to fifty million people worldwide were thought to have lost their lives to it. By now, no-one here was even mentioning something called Brexit, not even the Prime Minister. How we all longed for simpler days, like those.

Colin was a Police Officer. The Lockdown was not an easy one for him or for other officers based at his station in Nottingham. The challenge that they had was how to interpret the Government guidelines and instructions. And these changed over time, but also quite quickly. They had gone from recommendations to general guidelines and then from March 23rd to a formal Government Instruction, to the whole of the UK population. He listened to his immediate Boss talking to the local radio station one morning in a local Current Affairs programme where he was being asked exactly what the role of the Police was at this difficult time. His Commander explained that their role was to encourage people, and perhaps to educate them too, in order to change their behaviour. If we were all instructed to stay at Home wherever possible then people should do that but that also gave the Police the right to politely stop people who were walking about and ask them where they were going to. Many of them it turned out were legitimate NHS Workers going to or from their place of work, whilst others were out and about for a stroll and were encouraged to return to their home safely as soon as possible. Taking a daily form of exercise like walking or jogging was fine but it was recommended that doing this locally only was the right way to do it. Driving fifteen miles to a beautiful area of countryside to go and have a walk with your dog was not the way. That was an unnecessary journey and the dog should be walked locally to where you live. The work of Colin and his colleagues was made much easier if the Great British Public chose to behave responsibly in line with the Government Measures. That meant that there was little need if any for the Police to enforce at that point, and certainly imposing fines or arresting someone was the last thing that he or they wanted to do. He was called on a couple of occasions to form a group of officers that were needed to go and break up some large gatherings in the sun in the park one weekend in early April. He found it nearly unbelievable that people thought that could be acceptable. In one case there were over fifteen people having a sort of Summer Party out in the park, sitting right next to each other, and very definitely flouting the Social Distancing Measures. That one was politely broken up, but firmly too, and they were all sent home within minutes. His former colleagues down on the South Coast had been breaking up groups sitting on the beach in Brighton, one grouped around a beach barbecue, and again they had done that with courtesy but also as fast as was reasonably possible. They too were sent home. That said, he was not in agreement with what the Police Force had done up in Derbyshire in pouring a black substance of some kind in to the beautiful blue waters of a beauty spot in Derbyshire one weekend in order to deter visitors from visiting the beauty spot. That was going too far in his opinion. Other days had been very busy escorting Ambulances from and back to hospitals with urgent cases, as well as getting urgent medical supply vehicles safely escorted to where they were most needed. All in all it was a very strange time to be a Police Officer. At that point in time, he had not known of any of his Force Colleagues catching the virus.

For others, the Pandemic had been an economic disaster. For Markus a great StandUp Comedian, his Line of Business had been put on hold indefinitely. He was a clever guy and he used his time to be writing more material and to get on with a book that he had been writing on and off for some months. He was lucky that he could do some radio work too. But the land of people pouring into a Comedy Club on a Friday night, pint in hand, and sitting just feet away from other people, that really seemed a long way away now. He wondered when it would ever come back. In truth he wondered if it ever really would. After all, who was really going to feel that on one weekend you weren't safe in going to a gathering like that but that somehow magically the following weekend it was all suddenly quite different? What if you found yourself sitting next to someone who was sneezing or coughing during the evening? Were you really going to sit there out of politeness and not move, and not say anything, or were you literally going to jump out of his/her way as soon as you were physically able? Your politeness could mean the difference between catching the virus and not. And we had all come to know what that could mean, potentially. Nobody wanted to find themselves in an Intensive hospital ward like Jane's. With the greatest of respect to Jane and her dedicated colleagues.

Christine ran workshops for a living, delivering High Quality sessions on things like Management and Leadership. She worked with a range of Clients up and down the country and in many sectors, that included Technology, Telecomms, Consulting and Aerospace. She was very well regarded and she often won business through Word of Mouth recommendations. Simple but very effective. Like Markus, the bottom had fallen out of her market. More or less overnight. Ouch, this was very painful. The Time of Lockdown, well she likened that to driving off a cliff, because that is what happened to her business. Her earnings went from something like £5,000 a month down to less than £750 a month. She had suffered a drop in salary of around eighty five percent, and the real pain that there was no warning given. Like an Exocet missile, this had been fired out of the dark at her and there was no time to react.

Others found themselves in the same boat. Owners of Bars and Nightclubs felt like they had been hit by the very same missile. Owners of any kind of eating establishment had no choice but to close overnight. A lot of food went to waste that week, except when imaginative restaurant and coffee shop owners kindly got it taken across to grateful charities free of charge who would use it well. Perhaps some Homeless people ate very well for a few days that week. Good Luck to them. For they too would need large helpings of Luck in the forthcoming weeks and months.

Sabrine ran a nice little SpeedDating events company in the Surrey, Berkshire, and Sussex areas. She arranged other Business Networking and Conference events too but they all came to a grinding halt that same historic week in March. Boris Johnson was no longer her hero, not any more, but at the same time she understood the reality of the crisis and why he took the decision that he took to Lock Down the Nation.

So, did it hurt her business? You bet it did! She went from earning a little over £40,000 a year to nothing from April onwards. All of her Client engagements were cancelled with immediate effect by the Friday of that same week. People's future Hot Dates would go on hold immediately then. She would have to draw down on her savings from that month onwards, although that was never part of the plan. But as they say … "Necessity is The Mother of Invention". One of her friends, who shall we say was rather free and liberal with her body, also found that her stream of "Regulars" dried up around that time too. Shame, the cash had always come in handy. These were difficult times for many professions then.

One other very interesting and true story was that of Simon, who had built up a good business in the line of Car Valeting, but delivering really High Quality work. He had many regular Clients in the Berkshire area, with vehicles like Jaguars, Range Rovers, Bentleys and Porsches. You can imagine the high earning Clients that he had built up over the years perhaps, mainly men but some female clients too. Well, remember that cliff? That's where he found his business also got to just a few weeks later. Here's the interesting bit though. He had one client who stuck with him even during this crisis. He was a man in his early thirties who had won the lottery, literally, winning many millions of pounds one Winter's night. And he had moved into a large house and filled the driveway and the garage with seven highly expensive prestigious cars. Apparently, he was not a pleasant guy and he would scarcely acknowledge Stuart when he came round for the regular clean on his amazing high-performance vehicles. One weekend, he had told Stuart to give the new McLaren a clean but that he would need to move it out of the garage to do that.

"Here's the keys, and don't do an average job. You'll never own a car like this in your life!"

Not a nice man then, by all accounts. When Stuart started the car to move it, it sounded very rough and there was a terrible noise coming out of the rear of the engine. It turned out that mice had got into the engine bay of the car while the guy was away on holiday in Dubai, and they had made a nest inside the exhaust system of his car, filling it with nuts and fish food pellets inside. The noise at the back was the sound of the pellets and nuts being spat out of the exhaust system, which required the exclusive McLaren to go into the dealership to have the exhaust system stripped and cleaned professionally. True story and one that no doubt cost a decent sum of money. But then again he apparently had a lot of that. Unlike Stuart, for the Time of Lock Down was very harsh on him indeed, and suddenly too. His income dried up within a couple of weeks. Not what you want when you're approaching sixty, not really.

Alex worked in the IT Industry selling Memory and Storage Solutions to Clients in the Banking Sector. His time of Lock Down was pretty good and he actually earned more money than he usually did. You see, there was now a sudden shortage of Memory as Production Runs had been affected globally and so those companies that could provide solutions to the Big Banks now were in a good position. And his company had what you might call a warehouse full of the stuff, so they made hay while the Sun was shining. Financially, Lock Down was going well for Alex then. On the family side, his eighteen year old daughter Gracie had her driving lesson cancelled for an unknown period of time, but aside from that, he was not having a bad time. Her driving instructor Lee was now out of work then for however long the Lock Down remained in place too. It became clear that different people had different experiences under Lock Down.

Joanna was. She worked in a Care Home. This was an industry sector that felt that they had all been forgotten. The focus of the daily Government Briefings that started at 5 pm each day was all about what was happening in the Hospitals. And that was important but people were also in need of Support and Guidance in the Care Sector. On a very practical level, they were in need of Personal Protection Equipment here too, and it was not coming through. Matt Hancock the Health Secretary said that people were taking part in what he called "A Herculean Effort" to get millions of pieces of kit like Masks, Aprons and Gloves distributed nationally but all that Joanna knew was that her Care Home in Scarborough was not receiving it. When she had called up the Government's Help Line this is what she had been told:

"It is what it is. It's not going to change. Why don't you just accept that?" ….. before the phone was put down on her. Unbelievable. Explain that one to her Matt Hancock, please, with all of your amazing figures of Distribution, Logistics and impressive local Deliveries. Wherever the lorries were going, they weren't reaching the Care Home where Joanna worked up in lovely Scarborough. Twelve residents in her Care Home died of COVID 19 over Easter as the virus did its dreadful work. More were seriously ill with the virus too. And that was just the residents, before the hard working staff are even taken into account. So, that was how Joanna's Lock Down was.

Teachers weren't really sure what to make of Lock Down. It had all happened so quickly. The next steps for many of their pupils seem to be in their hands now and to depend on what grades the Teaching Staff thought were fair estimates of their students' progress. At this point in the Academic Year there wasn't much else that could be done, other than base pupils' grades on recent past performances. That did have a reasonable logic to it. Some schools were able to run online classes for their students and from some accounts these were going quite well. Not surprisingly some Members of Staff found this easier to run with than others. After the Pandemic perhaps this kind of Learning might become more common. Nithan was just a few years into his Teaching Career and he liked running some sessions this way. Science was his subject and he found that he could cover good ground with a decent one or two hour session, and the kids then liked to be given a twenty minute break. They were fast establishing a good little routine in his Science lessons. He was fine taking questions online from pupils and then choosing when and how to answer the questions in such a way that the whole group got the benefit. That worked okay for his groups, or it had done so far. Yes, teaching remotely was okay for him and he would probably offer to do more and more of this going forward. His generation dealt well with it. Some staff were very upset that they might not see some of their pupils again if the rest of the Academic Year was cancelled. And just like the Football season, that was looking like a very distinct possibility. From the professional point of view they would also miss the satisfaction of taking their pupils up to a good level of attainment, and for some who were close to Professional Retirement that really would hurt. They felt that they had had something taken away from them, but at the same time they knew that people nationally were having their Life taken from them too. They were just sad at the overall situation, it went against the whole Ethos and the Purpose of a nurturing place, that was a school.

Ahmed worked for a well-known delivery company. They may possibly have a yellow and red logo and have a lot of yellow and red vans that drive around the country, at all times of the day and night. It's a company that would be familiar to you. How was his Lock Down? Well, he'd never worked so hard in his life! He was being offered extra hours and anything over his official 7.5 hours a day attracted "Time and a Half" rates. So after that point his hourly rate went up from £20 an hour to £30, for doing basically the same delivery work. This was a system that he liked! Very much. When the wretched Pandemic was over he would take his fiancée Sonia on that great holiday that he had promised her for so long. He had also been asked to help train a lot of the New Recruits that they had taken on and he got a few hundred extra pounds in his wage packet for making an effort here to take the new guys through the systems that they used. Business was very good, and they were getting more and more delivery business through companies that couldn't cope with their own levels of business. So they would bring the other firm in on the deal and deliver packages for companies like Amazon and some food companies too by using a new and temporary "Partner". It kept the Customer happy as their deliveries were made on time and everyone shared in the spoils. The margins were less but at times like this you have to make the most of a difficult time and the levels of business overall were really good. Consistent too, so Ahmed was happy. His one concern though was that back at base, in the Head Office and in the warehouse, they were rarely able to follow Social Distancing Measures, it just wasn't that kind of environment. So he had gone out and bought some packs of gloves and face masks out of his own earnings and shared them around, which had been much appreciated. His attitude was noted and several months later he would receive a promotion to a Regional Manager position. Who says hard work doesn't pay off? Not Ahmed!

Mavis works in a charity shop. Or rather she used to. She worked part time there and got a very small Monthly amount for her time but she enjoyed the work and it gave her a sense of purpose after Alfred had passed away. The Death Certificate that he had died of Pneumonia, but she knew that his symptoms had been that of a High temperature, a dry cough and a sense of being very tired. Alfred had never been a smoker, he was a very keen walker and gardener, yet in the last few days of his life he had experienced breathing difficulties. That was only a few months ago, in between Christmas and The New Year. The past few months had been very hard for Mavis, as she came to terms with his passing on. Going into a place of work was one of the ways in which she dealt with it, and learned to cope in her own way. Both of their children lived overseas and by now they had their own families. They also had their own lives too, so work was doubly important to her. It was all she had. So you can guess the impact of the Lock Down on her, and how that affected her daily routine. She had done bar work and some Light Accounting too over the years but since everywhere was under Lock Down she would just have to be patient. Until then she would stay at home, doing this and that around their pleasant enough garden, and looking at her husband's Death Certificate ….. wondering what had really taken her Alfred away from her, for good. Those symptoms seemed awfully familiar.

Boris stood outside Number 10. on the Thursday evening, to acknowledge the fine work of the NHS staff. He wasn't at his best having caught the virus himself. He had posted a Tweet that he had a temperature and a dry cough, and that his Doctor had advised him to self-isolate for about a week. Just like Matt Hancock his Health Secretary had done, and look how quickly he was back at work, all well and recovered. So the Prime Minister would be fine too. At eight pm he was out there on the steps of Number 10 clapping vigorously in support of the NHS. They were capable of saving people's lives you know, they were that good in the British NHS.

You didn't need to be an expert though that night to spot something…. Boris Johnson, the Prime Minister was not looking at all well. We knew that he had been confirmed with the virus and that he had to self-isolate but he looked very rough. If a Prime Minister can look rough, then he did. He was wearing what looked like a navy blue suit, and a pale blue shirt. He had no tie on at this late point in the evening and he had a wristwatch with a brown leather strap on his left hand. He appeared to be standing there applauding, like much of the country was at that time, but a sharp eye would see that he was holding back. He wasn't leaning against the door frame but it did look like he nearly was and that he wanted to stay close to it, on his left as he looked out. In case he needed to lean against it for support. He looked sweaty and his facial expression looked what you might call "Pained". He was clearly suffering, like anyone who has the symptoms of something like flu. At one point he takes a step forward in the door frame to look out and up Downing Street a little to his left, perhaps to see something further up the short road, maybe looking towards gates perhaps. Once he can go back in though, he does, waving to the Press that may have been still outside No. 10 and in he goes. This was not the Boris Johnson that we knew, this was not Tigger at his best.

The rest we know. On Monday 6th April, he went into hospital. Boris Johnson would then spend several nights in intensive care after his coronavirus symptoms worsened, and overall charge of the government was handed to Dominic Raab, the Foreign Secretary. In an unprecedented development during a public health crisis, the prime minister was moved to intensive care at St Thomas' hospital, London, at 7pm on that Monday night as a precaution in case he needed ventilation, it was said. He remained conscious on Monday night.

A No 10 spokesman said:

"Over the course of this afternoon, the condition of the prime minister has worsened and, on the advice of his medical team, he has been moved to the intensive care unit at the hospital."

We don't know all of the details of his stay in hospital, nor should we, but we learned that "it could have gone either way". Boris Johnson thanked the NHS for saving his life as he left hospital to recuperate at Chequers, after a week of treatment for Covid-19. He praised two nurses in particular for watching over his bedside in intensive care for forty eight hours hours "when things could have gone either way" – Jenny from New Zealand and Luis from Portugal. Speaking in a video message just hours after leaving St Thomas' hospital in south London, the prime minister expressed optimism the UK was "making progress in this incredible national battle against coronavirus". Johnson said he had left hospital "after a week in which the NHS has saved my life, no question". He said the country was mourning "every day those who are taken from us in such numbers, and the struggle is by no means over" but he argued progress was being made "because the British public formed a human shield around this country's greatest national asset – our NHS".

Johnson said he had seen the pressures the NHS was under after seven days in hospital, including three in intensive care. And he had witnessed the "personal courage not just of the doctors and nurses but of everyone: the cleaners, the cooks, the healthcare workers of every description, physios, radiographers, pharmacists".

Boris would return to work at some point, when his Medical Team allowed him to.

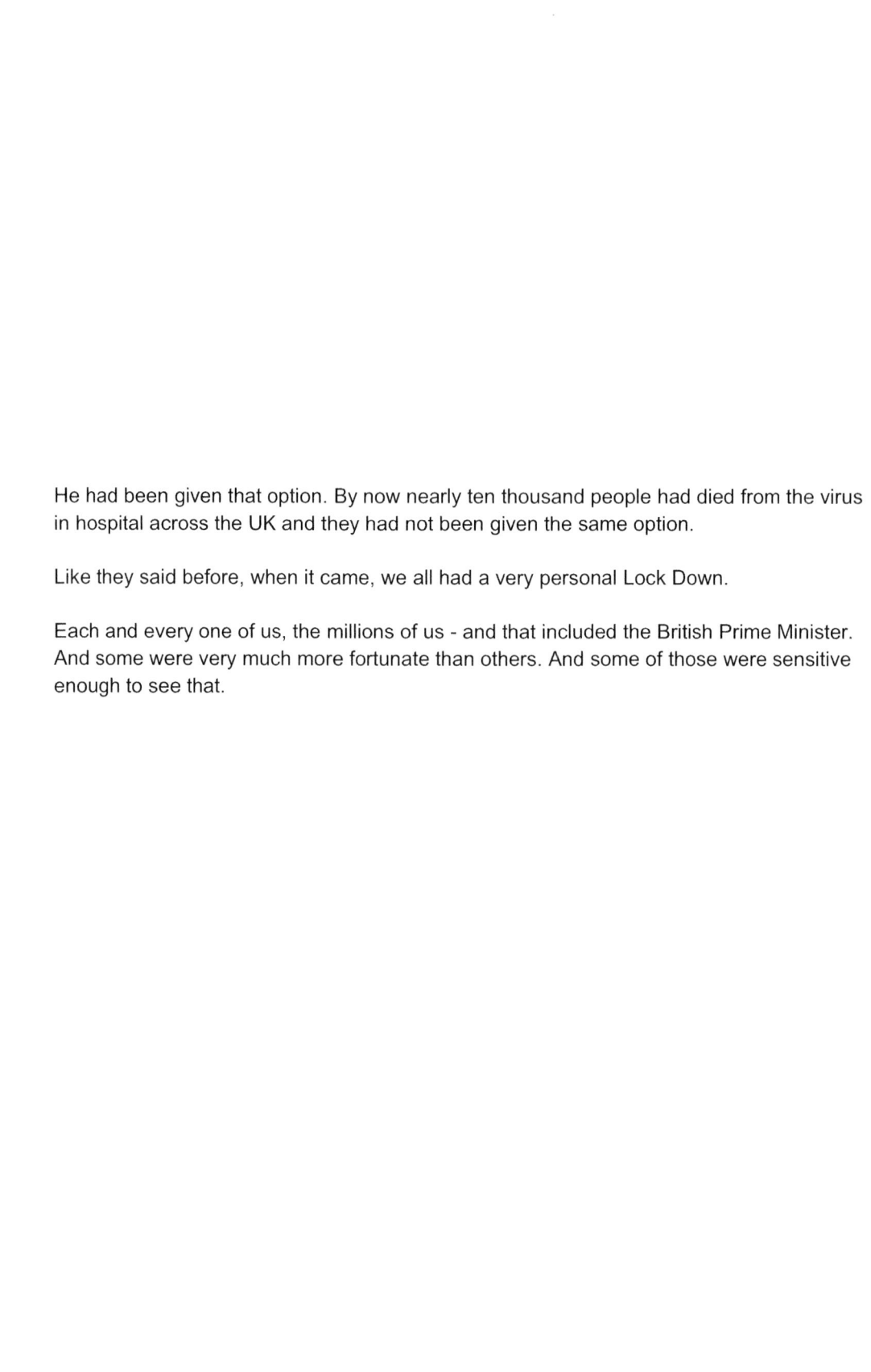

He had been given that option. By now nearly ten thousand people had died from the virus in hospital across the UK and they had not been given the same option.

Like they said before, when it came, we all had a very personal Lock Down.

Each and every one of us, the millions of us - and that included the British Prime Minister. And some were very much more fortunate than others. And some of those were sensitive enough to see that.

Printed in Great Britain
by Amazon